BETTY BLAKE, CHILDHOOD SLEUTH

Complete and Unabridged

LINFORD
Leicester

First published in Great Britain

First Linford Edition
published 2019

A catalogue record for this book is available
from the British Library.

ISBN 978–1–4448–4146–6

Published by
F. A. Thorpe (Publishing)
Anstey, Leicestershire

Set by Words & Graphics Ltd.
Anstey, Leicestershire
Printed and bound in Great Britain by
T. J. International Ltd., Padstow, Cornwall

This book is printed on acid-free paper

*For Mum
and my aunts*

BETTY BLAKE
CHILDHOOD SLEUTH

Featuring an amazingly perceptive Edwardian child blessed with a talent for solving village puzzles, Betty Blake provides us with a glimpse of a future amateur detective in the making. Betty begins her sleuthing at age nine continuing through to age twelve. Her cases include pillar box puzzles to headless ducks, a stolen emerald ring and the death of a solicitor's wife — not to mention a ghostly disturbance on a golf course. For someone so young and precocious— no case is a burden or unsolvable!

These three lucky children always had everything they needed; pretty clothes, good fires, a lovely nursery with heaps of toys and a Mother Goose wallpaper.

E. Nesbit
The Railway Children

Contents

NINE YEARS OLD

The Saucepan Mystery

Aunt Medley, Edwina Blake and Betty were sat around the table in the parlour about to start tea when Mrs Blake exclaimed surprisingly: 'Who burnt my saucepan? It's got a hole in the bottom. I came back from the shops and there it was on the range. I remember quite clearly washing it up in soft soap at lunchtime after boiling some milk; it was spick and span, good and shiny.'

'Well, dearest,' said Aunt Medley, choosing a cucumber sandwich, putting it meticulously upon her plate. 'Betty's been at school. I have been at Lyminster doing flowers for the church. I got back *after* you.' Both women scrutinised the child suspiciously.

'Don't look at me so, please,' said Betty. 'It's not my fault, it's really not. I can see the daft old saucepan from here; it is burnt black, but not by me.'

'Then who was it burnt the saucepan if none of us?'

Betty decided that after tea, before doing her homework for her teacher, Miss Tern, at the school house, she would look more closely into this mystery to put mother's mind at rest. A risible enough puzzle, but a puzzler just the same. Aunt Medley was going out into the garden to clear the bird table of any remaining scraps which at night tended to attract four-legged scavengers such as foxes, stoats and weasels . . . or rats.

Thus, Betty, after buttoning up her winter coat, allowing aunt to fuss over her woolly hat snatched from the peg and mittens from her coat pocket, went out into the garden. The snow lay settled, the low temperature keeping the surface, the crust, hard and firm. Together they went up the path which had received a scattering of coal fire cinders collected in a bucket. Even from the glow of the storm lantern the perceptive child saw quite clearly a rogue set of footprints leading across the lawn.

'Odd.'

'What's odd, dear?'

'Nothing much, auntie.'

However, young Miss Blake's sharp eye realised quickly enough one footprint was more deeply embedded than the other, more weight applied on the foot, the footprints leading away in the snow different; one had a chunky sole, the other more like a shoe, the tread of a lighter pattern: in plain words, *odd shoes, not a pair*. Well, who normally wears different shoes to walk about?

Whilst her aunt tidied the bird table, the girl, using her bicycle lamp for light, traced the oddly matching footprints over to a flower bed behind which was a wild bracken hedge that ran beside Prudies Lane. Someone, even an animal perhaps, had recently created a ragged gap roughly parting the foliage, bending and snapping twigs.

'Do come on, dear, it's far too cold to be hanging about. Botheration, where are you? What on earth are you up to now? Betty, answer me, don't dither, child.'

'Coming,' Betty said obediently, trudging over the snowy lawn, clasping her aunt's hand in hers and walking back to the house. The bright, hissing glow of the hurricane lamp warmed her cheeks, yet a far warmer glow filled her from within, for she was that little bit nearer to solving the saucepan mystery and, importantly, growing more and more confident in her own ability to search out clues.

★   ★   ★

Next morning at breakfast, Betty happily ate her boiled egg and toast soldiers, but her mother was still perplexed about the burnt saucepan and would go on. 'Leaving the pan on the hob to boil too long, forgetful, boiling potatoes, you see the heat and soot blackening the outside, water evaporates causing damage to the base.'

'Well,' said Aunt Medley full of admiration, 'Betty has solved the mystery, haven't you, dear? You told me while I was applying tooth powder upstairs.'

'Why, I believe it was Betty who burnt my saucepan,' accused Mrs Blake, pouring out more tea for everybody. 'You can't pull the wool over my eyes, dear.'

'Mother, really, it is no use blaming me, for it was Mr Stumpy who is responsible.'

'The gypsy over at the encampment?' Edwina Blake frowned, at a complete loss.

'Mended a chair leg for you, sat on the kitchen step smoking his clay pipe; you gave him sixpence last summer.'

'I did, too, but what does that grimy, smelly old man have to do with my saucepan?'

'When having his mug of tea that Saturday, mother, he must have glimpsed your pan boiling on the hob and taken quite a liking to it. They are both the same shape and size after all.'

'Tell your mama how it was done. Don't shilly-shally,' insisted Aunt Medley, cutting up her bacon. The girl, dipping her toast soldier into the orange egg yolk took a delicious bite before continuing.

'The footsteps in the snow; you see, Mr Stumpy wanted to hide his wooden leg so he would not be suspected. He slipped on an India-rubber wellington over the timber toe and came across from the caravans after he saw you hurrying down the lane to the village shops. He came across with his old, filthy, burnt saucepan wanting to replace his useless horrid one with your nice clean one — and he did. Mr Stumpy unlatched the back door and got in that way after cutting across the garden.'

The Sweet Shop Murders

'I want your finest chocolate cigar, please,' demanded Alfred Lloyd Clarke whose father was lord of the manor hereabouts. For now, like Betty, the boy was taught at the village schoolhouse, being often nicknamed 'Lord Snooty' on account of his upper crust, aloof manner. He was a most tempting punch bag for bullies, but even as a nine-year-old, he was a first-class, bare-knuckle boxer, so never bothered by them.

'There has been a frightful murder,' said Mrs Staple, who was proprietor of the village sweet shop.

'Oh,' said Betty curiously, her voice guarded. 'Do tell.' The girl chose a half dozen lemon drops for her own after-school treat.

'Terrible, awful it were, the head all cracked.'

'More details,' sighed Lloyd Clarke, unwrapping the foil from his plain chocolate cigar.

'Well, it were like I says. I come down 'ere to open up when I seen a chocolate rabbit had his head all smashed in, lying on the floor he were; my Easter stock, see?'

'How absolutely horrid,' sneered the boy offering Betty a withering glance before stepping out of the shop into the sunshine to join his pals, a wagonette and a buggy trotting past.

'It'll be the third to be done away with in that manner,' Mrs Staple murmured.

'All chocolate rabbits?' asked the girl, helping herself to a sweet from the bag.

'Aye, what's to be done, Miss Betty? I'm mystified, I really am.'

It must be admitted, young Miss Blake was up for the challenge since that winter so brilliantly solving *the saucepan mystery*, offering a very plausible and rational explanation that the village constable no less should have been hard put to equal. She was always happy when an opportunity arose to test her.

I mean, chocolate rabbits, for goodness' sake. Mrs Staple was widely regarded in the village as thick as two planks, a bit vacant, but there was promise here, potential to employ her wits to good advantage.

'If I solve this, Mrs Staple, I should quite like two free boxes of those Fry's mint creams: one for my Aunt Medley and one for mother.'

'Why, child, bless 'er. It shall be done. I'm losing stock, see. Allus can't stock killed chocolate rabbits with their heads bashed in, now can I?'

Before leaving with her bag of sweets, Betty noticed a *mouse trap* over the other side of the counter positioned along the skirting board, the wire engaged, a tiny scrape of cheese in place. High above, a narrow shelf ran along full of a row of chocolate rabbits. This prompted the little girl to call on Miss Nedlow whose cottage backed onto the shop, separated by a wall and garden in full riotous bloom. She walked briskly and in no time was using her balled fist to rap against the front door.

'Yes, Betty. What can I do, dear? Are your aunt and mother well?'

'Very. I wondered, Miss Nedlow, if I might earn a penny doing a gardening errand.'

'Such a kindness. I do have a little weeding in the flower borders needs doing and while you're about it, you might like to water the pots. You dip your can in the rusty water tank beside the glass house. You know how it's done by now. My servant, Molly, shall prepare lemonade.'

'Oh, thank you, Miss Nedlow.'

'Betty. Here, remove your ribboned school bonnet and put on this straw hat child, to protect you from the heat.'

The hot, clammy weather was in part responsible for the sweet shop murders, she thought, walking up the sunny garden.

At the end where the knapped flint wall was situated, she borrowed a wooden crate and, stood on tip-toe, was able to consider the view, taking into account the wide open rear windows of Mrs Staple's house across the way.

At night, because it was so humid, folk in the village, including the sweet shop owner, would keep their windows halfway or a quarter open to allow for cooling air. The parlour at the back led along the hall directly to the shop. A sill not too far up thus made it easily accessible.

* * *

'Goodness, this box of mint confection is really most thoughtful, and you say you solved three murders, all by the end of the afternoon. Shouldn't you have asked permission from Constable Johns at the police house first? Doesn't the local force at Wellingford normally deal with serious crime?'

'Betty, I'm delighted with my box of chocolate creams,' said her mother, proudly glancing up from her knitting, sat beside the homely hearth. 'I think you're very clever. Well, tell us child, what happened, who got arrested?'

'No one got arrested, exactly,' Betty answered, knelt beside her mother holding a ball of wool. 'I mean, you can't arrest a cat for chasing a mouse, can you?'

'Can't you, dear?' frowned Aunt Medley. 'A naughty one deserves to be.'

Jumble Trouble

Upon a spring morning in April, Aunt Medley unlatched the back door and brought in a cardboard grocery box full of odds and ends for the jumble sale. Faithful Mrs Appleton, the Blake's domestic, bustled from outside with another box, plonking hers on the kitchen table alongside the other.

The sale was taking place over at the village hall that Saturday at ten. The Reverend Smithson, who had only recently married Miss Caterham, was encouraging everyone at church to collect whatever — thus contributing to raising money for the church roof restoration fund — a very worthy cause because strips of lead were urgently required to stem the recent spate of leaks, preventing the need for rainwater-collecting buckets placed beneath the brass eagle lectern and stone font.

Betty Blake peeped into each box,

checking the selection of dingy contents on offer. A tatty china tea service, stack of picture frames, Mr Rodney's mantel clock with its back off, woollens, Mrs Lamb's old cat dish, worn dog lead and studded collar, a heap of women's periodicals, an old man's frayed coat with two buttons missing, donated by Joe Larch.

The girl went back upstairs to read her slim little beautiful Beatrix Potter book, biding time, for she had previously been commandeered by Aunt Medley for jumble sale service over at the village hall.

The village hall, where numerous activities took place, was built on a plot of land donated by Sir Winton Clarke. For instance, the Lyminster Dramatic Society held its plays here, the productions organised by Mrs Stacey, costumes made by Miss Lloyd and Mr Fernly Frith. The players were a social distraction that over the years provided residents young and old with a good deal of pleasure. This morning though the village hall was a hive of jumbling activity.

By ten, the jumble sale was in full swing; the hall was packed, card and trestle tables heaped with old junk, and during this first hour's clamour the hunt for bargains only intensified. Betty, who was selling ladies' hats, noticed a heated argument taking place on the stall opposite concerned with bric-a-brac between Mrs Rae and a gentleman wearing a shabby suit, spats and a bowler.

'Bloomin' sakes, I'se offered yer tuppence,' he said sullenly. 'Nows I says a shillin' woman and yer still refuses. Blast it all, 'ere's two bob. Now 'and the dish over. I'm being generous, I am.'

'Reserved — r-e-s-e-r-v-e-d,' she emphasised, taking no nonsense from this determined jumbler. 'My niece Val was in earlier and is to pay me a half-penny when she comes back from the shops, walking the baby with a pram.'

The man was flabbergasted and could not believe what he was hearing. 'Gawd save us, woman — favouritism. I'm offering yer more, not less. What's a halfpenny to two bob for a blasted ole dish what's cracked?'

'That dish is reserved for my niece and

that's an end. You realise we have a nearly complete tea service over here; plenty of dishes in better condition than that old cat dish.'

'That wuzz the one for me,' he sighed, no match for the woman. 'I tell you what, love, I'll take the teapot, cups and saucers. Can I get yer a cuppa over at the counter? There's not much of a queue at present. I'm gasping.' The man grinned, doffing his bowler, trying on the charm and succeeding.

'I will — two sugars, ta!' Mrs Rae replied gaily.

'An' a bun?'

'Certainly.'

'Thought any more 'bout my offer for the cat dish?' he struck a match and lit his cigarette, glancing at her slyly.

'No, I'll pack up the tea service for you in this newspaper. You just get on and fetch me my tea.'

The gentleman in the spats and bowler ambled across the hall to the kitchen cubby hole, the refreshment counter where was the tea urn, stacked plates, cups and saucers, sugar bowls and cutlery.

Talking of tea, Aunt Medley's friend Gertrude West on 'old furniture' came hurrying over to the used hat stall. She helped with flowers at the parish church, a cup of scalding hot fiendishly strong tea in either hand. 'The armchair and sofa's gone. You know with the chipped round table with the wobbly leg.'

'Oh, I am pleased,' gushed Betty's aunt, beaming from ear to ear. 'How much? Did they fetch the asking price?'

'A bit below, but that'll do. Reg, my husband, will undertake delivery later this afternoon to Mr Morton's cottage on the back of his wagonette.'

The girl was hardly listening, excitement over on the bric-a-brac stall opposite. Mrs Rae had fainted. The vicar and his wife crouched over, administering smelling salts.

The woman's eyes fluttered and she was soon on her feet, wondering what all the fuss was about, once more taking charge of her stall, while still more hordes of avid jumblers paid their admission at the door and entered the fray.

'Where's me dish?' demanded a young

woman barging through a throng of jumblers sorting woollens, using her pram as a battering ram, children in tow. 'Halfpenny, you promised, Ivy.'

'I've got it here, Val — least did 'ave. Now where in heavens name could it have got to? The cat dish was over here by the old carriage clocks. I even put a reserved label on it specially.'

'Excuse me,' exclaimed Aunt Medley, taking time out from making a display of ladies' hats.

'That man, the gentleman wearing the spats and bowler, the shabby suit?'

Val wheeled her pram aside, marshalling her children to allow the aunt through.

'I know the one,' exclaimed Mrs Rae, 't'was he who kindly fetched me a cup of tea. He forked out for the china service.'

'I think myself he was very deceitful and took the opportunity of pinching the cat dish when you fainted earlier. Betty, who was watching all the while, insists he may have poisoned your tea, adding powders. She saw him taking an awfully long time lingering over spooning in sugar. Betty hurried after him.'

'But what about my cat dish?' moaned Val.

⋆ ⋆ ⋆

Betty Blake was keen to identify the dish stealer and saw him for definite enter the high street antiques shop, making earnest conversation with the pompous proprietor Mr Veriker. The manager stood behind the glass counter wearing his frock coat and a red carnation buttonhole.

The girl pushed open the door to the shop; the bell pinged. 'Yes, what do you want child, can't you see I'm busy?'

'I'm ever so sorry, Mr Veriker, but that cat dish belongs to bric-a-brac at the jumble sale. It was reserved for Mrs Rae's niece Valerie, to be sold for helping towards the church roof restoration fund.'

The man sneered. 'I ain't a-caring for what this little toady says. It's mine, I told you, I got it fair 'n square see at the jumble sale orf a very nice lady, I did.'

'You put something in her tea to make her dizzy and faint,' said Betty, confident she was in the right and knew what she was saying.

'Stoppid toady — lies, lies.'

The manager, a fine upstanding fellow in the community, sided with the girl.

'I refuse to hand this item back to you, sir. Am I to alert our local constable, P.C. Johns? Look sharp, young Mr Levenson — hat, coat and stick m'lad. Fast as you can down to the church hall. Hup, hup.'

'Alright, alright,' said the nasty gentleman. 'I'm orf, I'm art of 'ere. Why you little toady, you.' He shook his fist at the little girl, tearing across the high street to board an omnibus to make a quick departure.

'My name is Betty Blake, actually,' she cried after him, running to the door, very red in the face, indignant of his coarse and vulgar attitude.

'My dear young lady,' crooned the antiques dealer, indicating his assistant should bother himself no more in the apprehension of this villainous rascal. 'Inform the vicar at once that this item is no mere cat dish, but rare Ming dynasty porcelain worth many thousands of pounds. I believe the church shall face no problems of a leaking roof in future, and much more restoration work may be done besides, including the planned extension to the village hall, the dressing room area for the stage I heard mention of from Mrs Stacey.'

The Golf Course Puzzle

'The ghost of Major Smith on the golf course has got everybody talking,' said Aunt Medley, helping herself to a muffin and buttering it lavishly. She chomped for a bit, adding, 'Why, oh why should his ghost appear so soon *after the funeral* where the links run along by the cliff path? Why not in the club house or at a particular bunker, or teeing off point? The major was a stalwart member of the Seahaven Club for years. He must have played countless rounds of golf. I am not really very conversant with the game; you and Penelope Lunt play, don't you darling?' Betty's mother merely nodded, sipping her Earl Grey quietly, not really wishing to become involved.

'Don't you see, it was *after the funeral* that is interesting,' explained the little girl, Betty Blake, her eyes bright and questioning.

'I can tell you're in one of your 'clever

clogs' moods, about to deliver a stunning blow on behalf of puzzles. All I can tell you is that the ghost of Major Smith has been seen on a number of occasions by golfers returning to the club house at eventide when the village church clock strikes the hour. Our padre refused to comment in this week's parish magazine, despite I and a lot of Sunday worshippers raising the issue. I mean, something had better be done, surely!'

'Done? What's to be done?' enquired mother, cradling her teacup, elbows on the table cloth.

'Why, to exorcise this ghost, send him packing off the links in a puff of smoke.'

The little girl found this adult talk distracting from the key issue. 'Listen, Auntie, Mummy, a week or so back I saw a firework, a rocket, shoot up into the sky over the golf course from my bedroom window. It was very early. I know my alarm clock said twenty past six.'

'A firework? But it's not November, dear, it's only August.' Polishing off her first muffin, Aunt Medley hastily buttered another, her brow furrowed.

'I told Miss Tern at the schoolhouse about the rocket; she was so very nice and suggested a distress flare might have gone up, a coastguard signal.'

'Very logical.'

'But Teacher couldn't recall reading in the local paper about a lifeboat being launched, a ship on the rocks, someone lost at sea.'

'Commendable.'

'So, after school, I and my best friend, Lizzie, set off along Coast Road on the horse bus to the golf club. I asked at the office and the club secretary, Mister . . . '

'Yes, Gervais Atkins, I know him,' said Edwina Blake feelingly. 'I hope you were polite, dear.'

'Yes, *we were*, but you see, Mummy, he told us all about the terrific send-off for Major Smith from his golfing pals.'

'You mean . . . oh, that's just too unconventional for words,' gasped Aunt Medley, beginning to twig on.

'They made a pact, you see, that when the time came, Major Smith's ashes should be mixed with gunpowder and spread about the golf links, the place he loved, where he had made so many friends over the years. They agreed on a simply super way of scattering his ashes, only . . . '

'Only what? Betty, please don't leave us on tenterhooks,' mother said with a twinkle in her eye.

'There was a bit of a breeze blowing and the rocket shot over the cliff, not over the links as planned. Well, I suppose no one but me thought of it, but the major was an army man, *not navy*. He wouldn't want to be buried out at sea, but fortunately I've an idea. If we can find the burnt rocket, there may be enough of his ashes left to help.'

'Where, oh where do you suggest we start looking? I mean, we're not about to hire a boat and cross to France, Betty.'

The little girl thought hard. 'Why, that cliff walk, the sea wall where everyone strolls on Sunday, near the tea and ices kiosk directly beneath the cliff. I think the rocket may have landed somewhere there. Mr Atkins showed me how the firework was blown off course using his hands.'

Remarkably, there was, still existing inside the cardboard tube of that spent rocket, the cone having blown up in flight, a mixture of ash. It was a Brock's Firefly with a long stick, but what remained had been forlornly kicked to the side of the concrete path along by the sea wall and lay amongst some rubbish. Mother was first to spot it and Betty went running over, nearly losing her hat, to pick it up.

After partaking of a glassed ice at the kiosk, the sun beating down, Aunt Medley, Betty and Mrs Blake went back up onto the Seahaven golf links and the little girl watched curiously the powdery, gritty ash being sprinkled about the tufty grass, the Brock's firework being snapped in two and squashed into a rabbit hole.

When Edwina Blake next played a round of golf with her friend, Penelope, she heard no mention of Major Smith's ghost in the club room, nor out on the course. Her friend pointed out, however, someone had scratched in chalk on the back of a memorial bench 'Thank you,

Betty', the work of who knows who, *probably* unrelated.

The Fat Policeman

P.C. Johns was the village constable who lived at the police house, a cob and thatch cottage opposite the Mitre Inn. Recently he had been in the papers for as Aunt Medley pointed out, he had been officially commended for bravery after arresting a house burglar, rather a violent cracksman called Alfie Nibbs who lived locally and had nine children, who was tried at Wellingford assizes and sent down for six years hard labour, the crook's wife having to be restrained in court after the verdict, the jury all of one accord, for she lashed out viciously at P.C. Johns with her handbag saying the unrepeatable. He suffered a bruised cheek, but did not press charges and let her off with a caution.

'He is rather on the fat side,' mentioned mother, darning a stocking in front of the cheery fire, a glass of sherry at her side, the banshee wind shrieking and howling outside, rain lashing in torrents against the latticed windows of the cottage they shared, for it was, after all, the end of October and well into autumn — a time for squally gales.

'What's fat got to do with it? He is young and a first rate community officer, and we are extremely lucky to have him as our village policeman. The last one, old P.C. Crewe, was thin and next to useless.'

'Well, sister dear, largely built, well rounded is what I meant, which reminds me . . . Betty, would you tomorrow before school, dear, providing the weather's cleared up, take some jars of home-made jam and pickle to the police house for the fat . . . I mean, P.C. Johns. He's always so generous with his ducks' eggs.'

'Lizzie and Mary Meredith, who live opposite to the Nibbs family, say the grandmother is a witch, Mummy. She owns a hazel twig broomstick and a big black cat.'

'A cuddly black cat makes for a fond pet,' laughed Aunt Medley. 'My, you should make a fine general to equal Mathew Hopkins. Are you to inform on

Grandma Nibbs, then? What is to become of people who own more than one big black cat?'

'The witch hazel broom is ideal for sweeping paths, dear,' her mother reminded. 'I'm surprised you are so quick to accuse, Betty . . . you'll need more evidence, surely.'

'I'm not accusing anybody,' sighed the little girl, 'but Lizzie is my best friend.'

★   ★   ★

The next morning, knocking at the front door of the policeman's cottage came no answer. Betty decided to pop round the side and leave the home made jam on the kitchen step. When she got there, the door was actually unlatched and part open, but no one about.

Glancing up the garden, apart from the duck house, the meandering stream and the well, she caught sight of a shingle-roofed shed where the fat policeman indulged his hobby for model railways. The foliage was wet and dripping after the night's windy weather, the path shiny with puddles. The door to the hut was ajar. Suddenly she remembered it was October 31st. The model railway took up most of the shed, laid out on a pair of large, flat pieces of plyboard. It had a country station of printed tin, a goods yard, tunnel and bridges. Much attention to detail had been lavished on painting and modelling the landscape out of papier mâché. Tiny-scale people inhabited the station platform, sheep grazed in fields, fencing, miniature hedgerow and trees all in place.

'Mr Johns,' she called out, feeling rather stupid for he was obviously not there, but sensing somehow someone was present in the shed. Then, out of the corner of her eye the girl could hardly believe what she saw — a tiny red flag waving frantically from the roof of the printed tin model signal box.

Astonishingly, the fat policeman was holding on for dear life to the chimney pot, one hand waving the flag. Although still tubby in stature, he was more of a 00 gauge fat policeman who appeared exactly the same scale as the lead figures of passengers on their bases waiting along the platform. In fact, the red flag had been purloined from the painted guard who now had a hole in his flesh-coloured fist.

But what interested the child, causing her to pause and reflect, was the smell of pipe smoke that permeated the air. P.C. Johns' favourite tobacco pipe, the bowl still warm to the touch, rested on a brass ash tray, this upon the wooden work-bench beside an upside-down, little, tin locomotive, its insides being fixed; a winding key, oil can and a smattering of screwdrivers indicated Mr Johns had been disturbed while working, his three-legged stool scraped back.

'What to do, what to do — the wicked grandma had something to do with this, *Alfie Nibbs' mother* protective of her son, vengeful because he had been imprisoned for six years hard labour, caught red-handed by P.C. Johns, sent down by the judge, leaving his wife to cope with nine children,' Betty thought desperately, screwed her eyes tightly shut then opened them again with a start.

The shoe box; that item had not been there, under the trestle table when she last came to visit in August with Aunt Medley, the kindly officer showing off his little prize model railway. P.C. Johns was normally tidy, everything in its place, and this helped because the shoe box certainly seemed out of place, definitely so.

Ignoring the roof of the metal signal box where the miniature P.C. Johns still waved his flag frantically, Betty knelt down, carefully prising open the cardboard lid. So! It was the grandma after all. Her school friend Lizzie had been right all along. Now for the hard evidence.

There inside, nestling on tissue paper, was a doll dressed up like a policeman, the uniform painstakingly stitched together, the helmet accurate even down to the county badge; the doll made in the image of P.C. Johns had six hat pins stuck in it. Beside the doll was a brown glass bottle containing horrid liquid, bits of stag beetle floating about in the murky solution.

The girl needed no prompting; she ran out of the shed and threw the bottle to the ground, dashing it to pieces on the flagstone path. She hurried back to the hut and, kneeling down, one by one removed each sharp pin from the doll, careful not to prick herself.

P.C. Johns rapidly grew back to normal size, but too fast for his sheer weight and bulk meant he collapsed the plyboard table, squashing his model railway.

The Tinker Caravan Case

Breakfast finished, the schoolhouse closed for the holidays, Betty Blake was about to put on her straw bonnet and hurry off to visit her best friend, Lizzie Meredith, when a commotion occurred at the back door.

Mr Stumpy, a smelly tinker who hobbled along on a wooden leg and lived on the gypsy caravan site in Prudie Lane where resided the Romanies, whose smoky rubbish fires, litter, multitude of beggarly urchins and overbearing lucky heather ladies were the bane of the village, poaching game being another nuisance, bustled into mother's kitchen sobbing his heart out. Mama was a charitable soul and seeing the despairing state of Old Stumpy, left off her washing of an ornament in soft soap at the sink to find out what was the matter.

'Lor', Mrs Blake,' he gasped, tears streaking his grubby face. 'It were just too 'orrible fer words, just too disgustin'. I'm afeared to go back there, but I must. A curse, that Grandma Nibbs at the devil's own work agin, just mebbe coz I done her for a couple o' shillin' over some rabbits. I picked 'em up, run over by the roadside — definitely fresh they wuzz. Now this! Gawd strewth what's to be done?'

'Do calm down Mr Stumpy,' urged mother, trying to ignore his astringent pong. 'Just take a deep breath. Now where's that old enamel mug got to?' (The one she used for rinsing her paint brushes, reserved especially for 'rough and ready' types like Stumpy or the knife grinder Mr Saddler). 'I'll pour you some tea and just talk us through it. Too horrible you say.'

'Ta, disgustin', revoltin', all becuzz of tha' Lyminster witch whose son Alfie is the thief. Look, Mrs Blake, that hag done fer me alrigh' — worse than when she had it in fer P.C. Johns awhile back.'

Listening in the hall, the girl quickly removed her coat and put it back on the peg. She hurried to the kitchen where Aunt Medley sat serenely reading The

38

Times, her crossword puzzle pencil poised, not caring for, indeed snubbing if that is the right word, the very presence of the one-legged gypsy notorious in the neighbourhood for dodgy dealing and leading people on to part with their money for 'old tat' on the door-step. Mr Crebton came to mind, who was swindled out of a shilling to buy a useless blunt saw and broken screwdriver.

But Betty was intrigued, for what was it exactly that was so horrible for goodness sake, why was Mr Stumpy so upset? Aunt Medley continued with her crossword, she just had no time for the grubby tinker who smelt to high heaven of wood smoke and stale sweat, why his pair of filthy trousers could probably walk of their own accord they were so ingrained and shiny, stiff as ply-board with greasy grime. But the unshaven tinker did have a useful side, she supposed, mending chairs; and in the past he had made some fairly presentable basket-work when bothered. 'Fust,' said the old gypsy gratefully accepting his proffered mug of tea, 'I'se thought it were Sam Brinks what lives on the site, but then I remembers HER, ole Mrs Nibbs, Alfie's grandma, an' I knew — I knows it wuzz 'er.'

'Oh, for goodness sake,' sighed Aunt Medley, 'explain yourself in proper English. What is Mrs Nibbs supposed to have done? What are you accusing her of, Mr Stumpy?'

The girl added excitedly, 'Oh, please tell us.'

'Well Betty, it were maggots. This morn I seez a pair o' wrigglers peepin' out of the carpet, the pile, like, so then I'se rolled back the carpet. The underlay was alive wiv 'undreds of 'em, and then I'se sicked up. Couldn't 'elp meself. The sight of all them mass of 'orrible, 'orrible wriggling maggots writhing about in me very own caravan. I sicked up, I done. To think when I wuzz justly sleepin' in me bunk all that lot wuzz undulatin' in me carpet — more and more of 'em.'

'Oh, 'ow awful!' said the domestic, screwing up her face in disgust. Everyone in the parlour agreed it was pretty shocking to find maggots wriggling in your carpet first thing in the morning.

But was that because of a witch's spiteful curse? Betty knew Grandma Nibbs was the real deal, a black witch like you read about in scary fairy tales.

Drinking another mug of tea and being further fortified by a chunk of mother's home-made raisin toffee, doffing his greasy flat cap the one-legged gypsy took his leave. The worst must be confronted. Mr Stumpy knew he must hobble back to the camp, thence to bravely untack and lift out the roll of maggot infested carpet from his caravan, casting the ruined material, alive with undulating white pupae, into the flames of a roaring bonfire.

'Cursed,' he muttered, clumping down the garden path on his timber toe. 'Ol' Grandma Nibbs is to blame.'

★ ★ ★

After Mrs Appleton, the Blakes' faithful domestic, assisted Betty on with her coat, she straightened her bonnet in the hall stand mirror, a lumpen piece of oaken furniture, making preparations to take the dog for a walk and think things through. She decided before calling on Lizzie to visit the woodland area surrounding the gypsy encampment. Her woolly Scotch terrier should enjoy the run.

In no time they were crossing Prudie Lane, entering a leafy footpath attained by clambering over a five-barred gate. There could be viewed beyond the tangle of undergrowth, the evergreen wilderness of glimmering sunlight comprising knee high nettles, sedge, the encroaching low hanging branches of birch, ash and elm a circle of five gypsy caravans gaily painted, each with a stove-pipe chimney, shuttered window and timber steps leading up to the entrance door, these horse drawn cosy dwellings so favoured by Romany travellers. Mr Stumpy was busy tending a crackling bonfire, poking up the showers of sparks and flame, the horrid roll of maggoty carpet close by, about to be incinerated, so good riddance.

Aunt Medley did not as a rule favour gypsy folk but Betty Blake thought the menfolk free and boisterous, handsome bronzed fellows used to an outdoor life, sporting their jet black, shiny hair, gold earrings, proud of their horse fairs and way of life, the women and children confident in themselves, very much alive, if a tad unconventional to English village society.

Actually, in point of fact it was her adorable Scotch terrier who, scampering along the woodland way, came to a clearing and alerted the girl to certain brilliant possibilities. The dog paused to sniff its muzzle about the carcase of a dead pigeon lying on the path, its meaty breast torn out by a clever predatory hawk that soared from above to feed its young. The pigeon was partly decomposed and this gave Betty the answer to the maggot conundrum.

Quickly the girl and her little boisterous Scottie dog on a lead headed back the way they had come to find the gypsy encampment when she approached a group of gypsy children, kept well back, wearing bandanas, brightly and colourfully dressed, mothers tending a soot blackened cooking pot and a large size kettle above the flames of a wood fire, likewise suspicious. But her reason for visiting need never concern the Romany community, for she was about to put old Mr Stumpy to rights.

He was at the time poking at his bonfire, now a heap of smouldering grey ash, with a twig. 'Aye, what can I do for thee young Betty. Mum alrigh' be she?' He puffed on his clay pipe. 'Cuss the day I took them run over rabbits to the witch, cuss ta old Grandma Nibbs. True I done her fer a few bob child, but I neffer, effer deserved this. I sicked up I did. The ole hag sent me a plague o' maggots. God 'elp 'er twisted soul.'

'Excuse me,' said Betty, a trifle loftily. 'A witch's curse has nothing whatsoever to do with your maggots. Please Mr Stumpy, you yourself are the culprit — none other!'

'Er,' the elderly gypsy's countenance darkened considerably. 'I sicked up, are yeese taking me for a laff young lady? If so, I aint laffin none — no I b'aint.'

Betty quickly explained, holding her beloved pooch in her arms and stroking its woolly head. 'Mr Stumpy, you take the short cut from the village using the woodland way to reach your caravan site?'

'I duzz Betty, yuzz I duzz.'

'The tip of your false leg leaves a mark of the stump in the ground.'

'Er?'

'You can see the holes where it digs in.'

'Yuzz.'

'Well, some time last week you were walking along the woodland path and trod on the rotting carcase of a dead pigeon with your hobnail boot.'

'Did I?'

'And muck got stuck to the sole of your boot.'

'Lass Wednesday I coom back tha' way — yer righ', Betty, yer righ'.'

'So when you got back to your caravan you accidentally trod the muck into your carpet.'

'So I would ha'.'

'In the warmth from your nice pot-bellied stove, thousands of wriggly maggots started to hatch. They love the thick pile carpet very much. They love to eat it, live on it and burrow under it.'

'Burnt the cussed things on the fire, I done,' spat out the old gypsy.

TEN YEARS OLD

Visit to the Library

Tugging her timber toboggan through the snow by a cord, the metal runners scraping along Old Pasture Lane on a very wintry day, more snow fall expected, the sky above the hedgerow dull and overcast, young Miss Blake came to the High Street proper, eventually reaching the brushed and cindered steps of Lyminster Village Library. She unloaded a stack of books tied onto the back of her little sledge. Betty had loaned, amongst other titles, a copy of the new Beeton's Christmas annual, thrilled to discover a detective story by A.C. Doyle featuring a new hero, Sherlock Holmes.

Gathering the pile of books in her arms, a hunched-over old lady wearing furs and a hat hurried down the library steps leaning on a pair of rubber-tipped canes, sending a couple of Betty's books tumbling, which she had to pick up again.

'So sorry, child, so sorry,' was all the

woman muttered as she hurried off, walking a bit like a crab, digging her canes into the snowy crust for support. She manoeuvred awkwardly down the High Street, soon lost to view.

Once inside the library, the girl was to witness 'a scene' taking place over at the desk where a concerned Miss Pervis, the head librarian, was talking with her two juniors, Gwendoline and Alice, who looked put out.

'Oh, girls, who would do such a thing? Who would be so cruel?'

'Not us,' Alice retorted smartly. 'I can assure you, Miss Pervis, neither I nor Gwendoline were in any way responsible, juniors although we are.'

'Forgive me, I did not wish to imply . . . '

'I should hope not.'

'But, girls, this is the second such incidence. Why me, why me? The first time I nearly tripped over a big fat book, *The Old Curiosity Shop* by Charles Dickens, deliberately placed outside the staff room; deliberately, I say, oh yes it was left there by someone who meant me harm. By Jupiter, if it hadn't been for Mr Asher grabbing hold of my waist just in the nick of time, down I should have gone, flat on my face.'

'That's jolly awful,' said Betty, peering up sympathetically. 'Are you alright?'

'Bless you, little Betty, I am perfectly fit my dear, if a trifle shaken, for you see not ten minutes ago I was wheeling the book trolley along the aisle by the reference section, a massive volume of the *Encyclopaedia Britannica*, thousands of pages thick, a calf-bound edition, came hurtling down from the top shelf. I only just managed to step out of the way. If that book, I say, had struck me full force I might have been killed!'

'Are you not exaggerating?' queried Gwendoline, picking up a pile of overdue books, getting back to work. 'Could not, for instance, somebody, a member of the public, neglected to put the encyclopaedia back properly after use?' The junior librarian proceeded to open the covers of the top book on the pile only to break out into a fit of sneezing. 'Sneezing powder placed between pages, blown up into her face by the fluttering paper', Betty guessed to herself. The junior's eyes were streaming, her nose red.

'But we librarians must requisition steps to attain such a height. I do not even comprehend how it was done, but that heavy book up there was meant for me, alright. Gwen, for heavens' sake, stop sneezing. Here, take my handkerchief.'

'Might you show me exactly where the encyclopaedia came down?' asked the girl.

'Dear me,' Miss Pervis replied. 'I must get on. What use is it to you, Betty, anyhow? Why, didn't I say already, it happened over by the reference section? Oh, very well, come across and I'll show you, child.' Leaving the junior still convulsively sneezing, blowing her nose, her eyes red and watering profusely behind the desk, the two proceeded swiftly to the reference section.

The method by which the *Encyclopaedia Britannica* had been dislodged became easily clear to Betty. Peeking behind the tall bookcase, she noticed a long pole leaning against the far wall, normally used for opening and shutting flanged windows placed high up. Upon this instance, she judged correctly, employed to nudge the heavy encyclopaedia off its top perch, the villain hiding behind the bookcase able to coordinate his aim by listening out for Miss Pervis's footsteps and the squeaky wheels of the library cart, but it was gazing at the polished floor that provided a vital clue to this 'whodunnit'. *Stud marks* recently pressed into the brown linoleum.

★   ★   ★

Billy Tasker was barely nineteen, working as a labourer at Dale's Farm. A traction engine crushed his lower body causing permanent injury to his thigh. He normally supported himself by means of a crutch. He was a bitter, surly youth and was not appreciative whereupon entering his favourite lunchtime haunt, the Mitre Inn, a young girl wagging a charity collecting tin, looking very determined, asked abruptly, 'Was it you who tried to hurt Miss Pervis yesterday at the library? Put sneezing powder in the book? I recognised those big hobnail boots of yours, one of the steel toe caps splashed in black gloss from upset paint. That was a horrid thing to do, dressing up like an old lady in a wig and fur coat, using the canes with rubber tips.'

'Yeah. Me, I fink it were grand clever, I does. Get outta me way.'

'When you came down the library steps you were wearing big studded boots under your dress.'

'Wot's it to you? I ain't bowered wiv that stupid Lyminster library n'more. That toffee-nosed cow fined me two shillin, two blinkin' shillin' for overdue books. I ain't paying. Them lady librarians 'ad it in fer me. I neffer done nuffink overdue, see? I got charged wrong.'

'Two wrongs don't make a right,' answered the girl, primly. 'You'd best go and apologise. Miss Pervis, the head librarian, nearly got hurt by that encyclopaedia you pushed off the shelf with the window pole.'

'Tol' yer, I ain't bowered wiv the library

n'more. Any'ow, Sunday I'm moving to Wellingford, 'elp me uncle do repairs, so there, you blinkin' pest.'

The 11:31 to Wellingford

The branch station with its coal siding was situated just outside the village off the main Lyminster to Wellingford Road, the forecourt approached along a leafy lane bordered by hedgerow trees lit at night and early morning by a row of gas lamps. Beyond the wicker fence with tin advertisements for Lipton's and Wright's coal tar soap were the platforms. A train was in, waiting to depart.

The country station possessed a steep gabled roof with tall, angular chimneys, the frontage timber-clad presenting mullioned windows and at the front entrance a pair of bright, glossy brown doors adorned by big brass door knobs which led to the ticket hall. Along the platform from whose awning hung a two-sided wrought iron clock was the station master's office, the telegraph room, a parcels office in which tickets, date punch and booking records were housed and the waiting rooms.

'Zorry about that there Lunnon connection o' yours, zir; bit late. Step over the footbridge, this one's for Wellingford.'

A gentleman wearing a frock coat and topper dashed off up the platform to catch his train, a puffing engine approaching the gated level crossing someway distant. 'Ah, good mornin', Miss Medley, an' you too, Betty. A day to beez indoor 'n by the fire I reckon, bit of a nip in the air. Still, compartment'll be nice and warm. No, I'se insist, allow me to take your bag. Christmas shoppin' is we?'

Aunt Medley, returning the clipped tickets to her purse, nodded. 'I am myself after fine French lace and crinolines, Betty, a Beeton's children's annual at Stoate's book shop in town.'

'An' ladies, you'll get allus that 'n more, no doubt. Now, I'll just shut the carriage door for ye; departure on time, too.'

The Paddington bound London express arrived at the country station in a mass of engulfing steam and sooty smoke, passengers crossing the iron footbridge to connect with the stopping service to Wellingford. Once all were on board, with a shudder of clanking couplings, the train pulled out, soon rumbling past the crossing gates and signal box.

'*The Secret Adversary* — in that book you're reading and were telling me about last evening. Who was he, dear?'

'The vicar. It was a tough puzzler. Penfold Dimkins. I worked him out only in chapter fifteen.'

'I met your fat policeman, P.C. Johns, the other day. He complained of always getting cycle punctures. He had two to mend on the morning I was at the ironmongers. The pneumatic tyres of his touring bicycle are well enough pumped up properly to the correct tension then 'bang', just as he's riding along. No reason.'

Betty did not say anything, but she strongly suspected Alfie Nibb's grand-mother who the Meredith twins *and she* knew to be a witch, was at the heart of this mischief. P.C. Johns had been responsible for gaoling her son for six years hard labour, the policeman never forgiven by the family, and that's a wife, grandmother and nine feral children.

While the train lazily followed the branch out of Lyminster, Aunt Medley writing with a lead pencil stub concerned herself with doing *The Times* crossword. Betty herself, lulled by the constant clicketty-clack of the two-coach train peered out of the carriage window at the endlessly engrossing winter's scene, the backcloth of hills, the patchwork of arable fields, passing farmsteads, thatched cob cottages with smoking chimney pots, a red-brick inn, muddy lane bordered by hedgerow, trees winding along beside the track.

At the next station a cluster of Christmas trees was quickly unloaded from the guard's van. The porter hurried into the ticket hall, barely squeezing past the booth. Several metal churns waited on the platform to be put on board, fresh milk being sent to the town of Wellingford.

Betty saw it all from the train window. She knew the stopping service regularly carried, beside passengers, fruit and vegetables in season, calves, horses, bundles of newspapers, day-old chicks and all manner of goods, serving the country villages along the line.

The girl continued to watch the activity, her sharp curiosity missing nothing. While the train remained stationary, a friendly old gentleman known well to the Blakes made an appearance, entering the compartment, doffing his tweed cap and taking a seat. Suddenly he became very beetroot-faced and flustered.

'Why, Mr Tadworth, what a pleasure!'

'No it ain't, Miss Medley,' said he, frantically searching his waistcoat. 'I gorn lost my pocket watch. Oh lor', what a bind. Now where could it 'ave gone to?'

'I think one of the Christmas trees snatched it,' said Betty excitedly.

'My dear child, the watch is a solid gold repeater wot belonged to my grandpa. This be no sort of joke, y'know. Sentimental I is about that watch, very valuable an' all.'

'Mr Tadworth, when I was looking out of the window, I saw you come out of the ticket hall and brush past the porter bundled with a lot of fir trees. You know how springy and prickly the branches are. You must have caught yourself, the branches brushed against your waistcoat while the porter squeezed past, snaring your not properly fastened fob chain, yanking the watch out. Hurry, hurry, do call out before the train leaves!'

'Well I must say, either Betty is being terribly clever, or very, very naughty,' proposed Aunt Medley frowning in a bemused way at the kindly old gentleman sat next to her, but Mr Tadworth, not slow to take the initiative, slammed down the compartment window, tugging at the leather strap, yelling out at the top of his voice, 'Evans, Evans, 'fore you blow that whistle my lad, check somethin' for me, could you? There's a shillin' for your trouble.'

'Three minutes before the train departs, Mr Tadworth. What is it you want, sir?'

'Check them batch of Christmas trees in the ticket hall waiting for the delivery cart. Me fob watch mighta gort tangled, see.'

Sure enough, moments later the porter came bounding up clutching in his outstretched hand the said item.

'By 'Enry, like a yuletide bauble it were, sir . . . and now I'll take that shillin' off yer if I may.'

The Emerald Ring

One June afternoon at the village schoolhouse, Miss Tern, wearing her usual grey serge dress and shawl, was writing with a stick of chalk on the blackboard, squeaking letters. At the back of the class a boy, Bert Crouch, for most of the lesson gazing longingly out of the sunny schoolhouse window, thinking of ways to build a tree house, turned all of a sudden to the pupil occupying the next desk, whispering so as not to be overheard, gazing past the extinct coke burner, not stoked and lit at this season, the stove pipe chimney poking up to the ceiling.

'Betty, my ma thinks daft Mary Chaff stole an emerald ring once belonging to great grandmother. My ma wears the ring, but it's a bit small and squeezes her finger an' she just slips it off sometimes for a minute and puts it on the mantelpiece. I do think Mary Chaff stole the ring, too. Mum's given Mary until this evening to hand it back or else. The girl were in the room, see.'

The term 'village idiot' was used rarely by residents of Lyminster, but it must be emphasised Mary Chaff did have sawdust between her ears. She was fifty-eight with the mind of a child, a simpleton, a fat, frumpy individual with a gormless moon face and enormous cleft chin and frizzy, untamed mop of ginger hair, who wore drab, oversized smocks and sandals in all weathers and did not endear herself exactly when she galloped down the high street pinching people's posteriors.

'Emerald ring; daft Mary nicked it. Must 'ave.'

'Why *must* she have?' enquired Betty, scribbling a message in her exercise book to avoid detention from the class teacher, shoving it across for Bert's inspection and response.

'She were with her ma,' he scribbled quickly. 'We wuzz playing cards . . . Snap.'

'Where was Mary?' she wrote in the exercise book.

'Gazing at herself, the silly potty head,'

came the reply, 'in the mirror above the mantelpiece, making funny faces for ages, rubbery faces, you know, like Paul Fish does, but she must have been plotting all along.'

'But no one in the room was looking at her all the time.'

'Who'd be bothered? Like I say, the rest of us wuzz playing Snap. Then the girl, the maid, came in with the tea things an' the silly oaf guzzling her tea from that cup with the spout come to settle down round the card table hogging all the sandwiches.'

'What are you two children up to?' called out Miss Tern from behind her desk.

'Nothing, ma'am, jest asking to borrow a pencil,' lied Bert Crouch.

After school, Betty was invited, along with her best friend Lizzie, to go back and play at Bert's house. While in the garden, making sure no one saw her, Bert and Lizzie chasing a rabbit loose from its hutch preoccupied, she stooped down to pick up a little length of worm-like rubber elastic nestling in the weeds over by the wall. Peering for some time into the middle distance she saw there was an orchard of hoary old pear trees, a rough piece of ground and neighbouring row of cottages further afield, then the girl was dazzled by a twinkling foil wrapping picked out by the sun along the base of the clay brick wall and likewise retrieved this.

★   ★   ★

Fortuitously, she met daft Mary bumbling along the high street mumbling to herself, spittle drooling down her big, cleft chin. It was sad to see the normally friendly giantess looking so out of sorts.

'I wuzz accused, accused,' she mumbled woefully. 'Oh, muvver won't like it, but I neffer, effer stole no blinkin' ring. Dunno who dirrit mind, wish I did.'

'I'm sure you're telling the truth,' said Betty, stopping her dead. 'So there was no one else in the sitting room apart from your mother, Mrs Crouch and Bert?'

'Nuzz.'

'Mary, don't be such a *dumb witness*.

There *was* another person. Now this is really, really important. When that other person, the maid, came into the sitting room and laid out the tea things, was it she who poured tea into your special spout cup?'

'Yuzz.'

'Was it she who brought your teacup over to where you were stood by the mantelpiece?'

'Nuzz.'

'Who then?'

'Bert.'

'Next, do you like mint humbugs, Mary Chaff? Do you buy bags off Mrs Staple at the sweet shop?'

'Hates 'em. I likes froo' drops or Fry's peppermints.'

Seizing the simpleton in the floppy smock by the hand, both hurried off to keep Mary's appointment with Bert's mother. At the kitchen door, Mrs Crouch was surprised to see such a respectable girl as Miss Blake associated with a loutish thief who in her mind had betrayed her trust and behaved very badly, pinching great grandma's emerald ring off the mantelpiece while she made strange faces in the gilt mirror.

'So, what have you to say for yourself, Mary? Give it back this instance do yer hear, my girl? Or we're for the police house.'

Betty swiftly intervened in Miss Chaff's defence.

'Mrs Crouch, it was Bert all along. Your son stole the emerald ring. He snatched it when the maid went out and everyone got distracted. The maid was blocking your view of the mantelpiece. Mary, drinking hot tea, didn't notice. Later Bert went down the end of the garden and, using a catapult flicked it over the orchard to his school mate Henry Dobson who lives in one of those cottages. The boys both buy mint humbugs from the sweet shop, they sold it to Mr Galin at the jewellery shop, who also deals in second-hand trinkets and that's where you'll find it in one of the trays in his glass counter. I know, cos I went in and looked.'

A woman of integrity, fair-minded, who helped clean the brass and arrange flowers in church, Mrs Crouch had to admit this explanation had merit and must not be wholly dismissed.

'Betty Blake, well I never did. How clever. I'd never have thought it out myself, but I tell you when my servant was upstairs in Bert's room cleaning, she discovered a brand new fishing rod and tackle box under his bed by the potty and that did seem suspicious. You girls go into the garden and I'll fetch you a glass of lemon barley water. Just wait until that wretched boy gets back from the park. He'll be in for a regular hiding, he will.'

The Headless Ducks Case

Ducks' eggs were appreciated by folk in the village for their size and flavour, and P.C. Johns when he was first invested as the constable for Lyminster at the police house built a very sturdy, duck house for his brood of eleven. A little running stream meandered at the end of the garden. Eggs were soon forthcoming and he made a little income from selling his produce. The ducks would often be seen waddling around the garden in groups, quacking to each other.

The fat policeman invested much love and labour to start his egg business. However, at tea one day Aunt Medley presented some startling news.

'Betty, your mother . . . '

'Yes, aunt, what about her?' The girl buttered her scone, bright bars of sunlight striking the starched table cloth, making the cutlery gleam and twinkle.

'Well my dear, earlier this afternoon she

took some pots of home-made pickle over to the police house, but oh, heavens, the foulest of murders done. I can barely recite the details. Darling, you'd better tell her.'

Mother poured herself more tea, helping herself to sugar from the bowl, spooning it in. 'Well dear, I popped in round the back way, intending to leave the box of pickles on the kitchen step, when poor Mr Johns, your fat policeman . . . '

'Yes, I know who you mean, Mother.'

' . . . came puffing down the path barefoot, his tunic awry, blood spotted down the front of his collarless shirt. He was in a right old state, tearful and muttering to himself. I got him into the kitchen and, settling him down, he told me what had happened. First, there was no usual quacking from the duck house so he instinctively realised something was wrong. Going up the garden he was appalled to find the duck enclosure had been broken into. Tangled wire, ripped apart plyboard, but when Mr Johns peered inside he found all eleven ducks

71

were dead. Their heads had been viciously bitten off and each smothered in dirt . . . part buried, feathers everywhere.'

'One sympathises, the poor, poor man,' intoned Aunt Medley, her voice full of genuine pathos.

'Poor ducks, you mean,' said the little girl, frowning. 'So, Mama, it was a fox.'

'Not just any old fox, a mangy, diseased animal that P.C. Johns said had been recently seen prowling round the village, entering gardens, visiting dustbins. The murders, that is the wanton slaughter of every duck, had nothing whatsoever to do with genuine hunger or feeding of young, Betty. Mr Johns believes a form of distemper might have caused the fox to behave as a cruel killer, who murders for the fun of it, out of control, its mind unstable.'

'A danger to the village. This sick animal must be put down before it attacks again,' insisted Aunt Medley, passing Betty the gooseberry jam on a saucer.

'Well, the village constable regularly feeds on the back doorstep a lovely tame vixen who he calls 'Gertie' . . . saucers of milk, chops, scraps, and she is perfectly well behaved and a credit to her species, so not all foxes are bad, certainly not. But Johns is insistent. He is going to lay out bait and shoot this mangy fox on sight, even if he has to wait up all night. Like many men around here, he owns a hunting gun which he showed me, so watch out mangy old fox.'

'But,' thought Betty, 'no one is taking into account that the so reviled mangy old fox had a limp back leg and was, according to her school friend, Lizzie, not skittish, but quite tame and had started to visit the dustbins and back door of No. 8, a terraced, thatched cottage along Old Pasture Lane, belonging to the Carter family, whose son, Tommy, was a schoolboy Betty knew, his father the local cobbler, so something did not quite ring true here.

Before tea was even finished, young Miss Blake was determined to act. After completing her homework she retrieved her toy printing kit from a box beneath her bed, a slim alloy tin containing an inky pad, the idea being to slide various solid letters into the grooves of the rubber stamp to form words; but it was only the pad that she took with her downstairs.

Promising to be back in ten minutes, she walked briskly up Old Pasture Lane to Tommy's cottage. 'Tommy, you must do this for me,' she said breathlessly at the front door step beneath the hornbeam lantern in the porch. 'Can you try to put the mangy fox's front paw on the ink pad and then place his paw on this sheet of paper to make a readable print. Is that too difficult?'

'The poor old fox is a bit weak so we feed 'im up, see. Dad gives him a crust of bread soaked in a potion to try and cure the mange, which makes the fox a bit dopey for a while and he curls up in a cut-down grocery box I did special for him. Later at night he trots off into the garden I s'pose. I'm sure I can oblige.'

'Bring the piece of paper straight round to my house. Don't, whatever, delay!'

'Right ho, Betty, will do.'

★   ★   ★

74

'Well, I must say, Betty, how kind of you to feel so concerned on behalf of my poor old ducks. I've been out tonight with my gun but no sign of the mangy old critter so far. It's for the best, the fox needs to be put down with that serious distemper. But I was very, very upset over the loss of my ducks. Of course I will listen to what you have to say. You and Tommy come inside and I'll put the kettle on. How's yer ma and auntie?'

'Very well, thank you. Now Mr Johns, first we need to visit the duck house. Have you cleared up yet?'

'Only the feathers and duck carcasses, which I disposed of by digging a hole. There's still much to be done.'

'Are there likely to be any bloody paw prints, any marks on the planks and plyboard?'

'Yes, I think so. Let's go and check. Here, I'll unhook my bull's eye lamp, draw back the shade. Tommy, light it with a wax vesta, will you? I'll put my gun safely back in its case for the meantime.'

By comparing even a roughly inked paw print on Betty's sheet of paper with those dotted about the shed it was clear that the miscreant, the ruthless murderer of those eleven poor ducks was not the mangy old fox as first thought.

'And he limps, you say. Well, by shining the lamp about, the bloody paw prints are strong, more steady than the older fox, more likely to be . . . '

'The vixen you feed?'

'Or its mate,' muttered the fat policeman realising that by leaving out food for the pretty sleek vixen he might himself be partly guilty of attracting trouble.

The Pillar Box Puzzle

'Complaints, complaints,' remarked Aunt Medley slicing off the top of her breakfast egg with her knife. 'What is the local postal service, part of the greater, efficient whole, born of novelist Anthony Trollope, coming to? Our very own postman accused of being irresponsible, slack when transferring mail from the corner pillar box to his sack and thence the cart. Packages and letters left in the mud, trampled in after being posted in good faith. He denies all wrongdoing. What are we to make of the allegations?'

Mother poured her daughter Betty another cup of tea from the pot. Sighing deeply she replied, 'Oh ye of little faith in our village postman. Why, poor, dear Mr Stawks has done his rounds without any significant complaint for the last twenty years or more, the Leaf Lane pillar box recently become a popular issue. There is even a suggestion the post box is somehow itself able to spit out the mail — jinxed. We the locals post our stamped letters — 'it', the official pillar box, irresponsibly chooses to eject them, leaving mail littered all over the kerbside. According to some, an outrageous infamy! The Lyminster Echo is having a field day.'

'Likely some journalistic stunt being put up by a clever young hack to sell more copies of the local newspaper. Listen to this latest headline and I quote: 'Haunted Country Post Box — The Problem Escalates. Village in uproar, local vicar, the Rev Smithson chooses to post a crucifix rather than a letter. Witnesses claim green toxic smoke billows out of the mail box. Post office H.Q. in Wellingford bombarded with requests for its removal. You read it here first.' And guess what, Betty? I do believe people are actually taken in by what appears to be a scurrilous, orchestrated campaign.'

The girl nodded eagerly. 'But are letters posted by those of us who use the corner box actually at risk, mama? You have to admit, I mean the slot is awfully like a big greedy mouth.' Betty dipped her toasted soldier into egg yolk, smiling sweetly.

But carrying on from Betty, Mrs Appleton, the Blake's 'domestic', wiping her hands down the front of her pinafore, concerned with blacking the kitchen range, spoke earnestly of her own recent experience. 'See, I'se went to the pillar box Tuesday, I done. Ma'am, honest to God posted a letter to me sister in Dover. Now, coming back from the village shops, same way I'd come, well, I'll be — there it was, trodden in the dirt, allus wet and soaked, ink smudged, address barely legible along with a scattering of other folks' letters 'n cards. Only gone twenty minutes I wuzz, mind. When next I saw 'im I gave that postman an earful, I can tell thee. My 'usband pointed out the pillar box to be painted in the devil's own colour — red, 'possessed' he tells me. Possessed by an imp.'

Aunt Medley and Mama tried but failed to repress an intense fit of giggles. Gaiety and laughter won the day, but Betty Blake, a juvenile solver supremo such as she, blessed with a photographic memory, an inquiring mind, felt unable to resist the lure of the *pillar box puzzle* and was determined to make headway.

That evening, moonlight flooding, shimmering through the banked-up hedgerow trees on either side of the lane, the girl, wearing her sealskin hat fastened round her chin by elastic, her nifty cloak and buttoned boots for which a hook was required to do them up, took her adorable Scotch terrier, Bertie, for his usual walk, making a detour along by the corner. The dog was for a time on his best behaviour, tugging on his lead, but then for some inexplicable reason suddenly, upon approaching the pillar box, went berserk, barking and yapping, straining on its leash as though doggily anxious to protect his adored mistress. 'Woof Woof, grrrrr, yap, yap,' the bright harvest moon seemed to temporarily cloud over, allowing for a brief spell of shadowy darkness. A pair of slyly blinking yellow crocodile-like eyes were gazing malevolently from the post box, staring through the slot. A shuffling of parcel paper . . . then what followed was extraordinary for, from beneath the gloss painted dome an envelope slowly slithered out, dropping onto the dewy verge. But as the moon once more came into prominence something more happened to chill the blood of both dog and mistress alike.

A loud, ghastly cry issued from one of the nearby gardens. Not a baying wolf, God forbid, but best described sounding more like a child being strangled, yet Betty was soon able to regain her composure for the girl recalled how P.C. Johns once explained that this singular cry, was nothing but Reb the fox who, when calling out for his vixen made such an awful, bloodcurdling din. This was just nature, normal animal behaviour.

★ ★ ★

The next day, it so happened concerning a separate classroom project, Betty visited her library, heading for the local history section. After enquiring at the desk, a Miss Cooter, a junior, assisted the girl find a suitable reference volume concerning the county but more pertinently the village of Lyminster, that is, when the village as she, mama and Aunt Medley knew it today was barely conceived, a time as was soon revealed, much crueller and unforgiving than her own.

No proper roads, only rough tracks existed, fewer buildings, justice doled out severely. Searching the pages, sat at a little table, she came across an old map and her heart began to race. The girl excitedly traced her finger along an old Roman track where Leaf Lane would one day in the future exist. However, in the seventeenth century, crudely named 'Olde Gallows Way' clearly identified was where they once hung people, a gibbet positioned surely where the corner pillar box was presently situated. A gallows! Capital punishment then enforced brutally in front of a crowd of onlookers, a mere entertainment for all the family.

Certain names amongst the various condemned caught her attention. For instance, Jeb Tanner, fourteen years of age, a lad, hung for stealing a loaf of bread in 1694. *A mere loaf of bread* had cost him his life at such a tender age — barbaric!

Professor H.L. Lallington was the author of the book in question. He was a local historian concerned mostly with folklore who it so happened lived along Old Pasture Lane and Betty had seen him many times tending his roses or leaning on the front gate smoking his curved pipe, being distinctive if rather queer for the bowl was carved in the aspect of a leering gargoyle. In summer he generally wore a baggy white tropical suit and wide brimmed hat. Indoors he pottered about in a velvet smoking jacket and tasselled skull cap. Mother and Aunt Medley were invited on rare occasions to afternoon tea.

Luckily, the professor, regarded widely as eccentric, was unafraid of controversy, only too pleased to assist the young lady upon hearing her startling theory expressed on the doorstep. Based on an early map in one of his books he found her proposed argument both feasible and brilliant, for if as many thought the corner pillar box was indeed jinxed, governed by some dark magic, this was surely as good a reason as any. Thus with post office permission (the H.Q. were actually considering removing the box to Cow Lane), the professor, calling in Lyminster's local history and archaeological society, a tremendous discovery rocked the village, being the talk of locals for months to come, for beneath the foundations of the innocuous postal box were discovered the skeletal remains of a felon wrapped in rusty chains, together with a buried stump of a rotten wooden post still preserved due to the acidity of the soil. As a direct consequence the Padre, the Rev Smithson, consented to give the bones a decent burial in the parish churchyard; thereafter the postal box behaved itself. Mr Stawks did not lose his customers' confidence, nor his job, and normal postal service was resumed to everyone's satisfaction.

The Locked Room Mystery

'How was it done?' asked the exasperated bank manager, Mr Herbert Andrews, offering a plate of pastry fruit tartlets for the delectation of Aunt Medley and Betty who were sat round his table at the tea rooms along the high street, which was as usual quite crowded and buzzing with conversation, mostly ladies' gossip. Mr Andrews was a church member who sang bass in the choir, hence they were friends.

'My light grey frock coat was ruined and looked unsightly, spotted with ink, but the room was locked, I say, the windows barred. I was sat at my desk alone dealing with a large deposit of cash, no-one else in the room apart from myself, so how did the darned ink spots get there? How exactly was it done?'

'A puzzler to be sure,' admitted the aunt. 'Alas, my own intellect should be found wanting considering this business of ink spots, but Betty, my niece, might be better able to find an explanation. She is rather clever at mysteries, aren't you dear?'

'Indeed,' the fellow butted in. 'I am assured of your reputation, Miss Blake: 'The Saucepan Mystery', 'The Sweet Shop Murders', and 'The Christmas Tree Felony' being amongst your early successes,' agreed the bank manager smugly, ingratiating himself. 'And yet this matter of my ruined frock coat may yet prove too formidable. Your age I refer to; you are but a juvenile.'

'I don't think so,' said Betty, daintily placing a fruit tartlet in her mouth.

'You don't think so,' said he doubtfully. 'Well I, an adult, just have no idea. All I know is that when I walked into the room my frock coat was impeccably clean and pressed and when I came back out again bank staff were sniggering behind my back. My head clerk Mr Dunn pointed out the stains; we thus sought out the cloakroom's full length mirror.'

'But Mr Andrews you're absolutely

certain the ink spots were not there before you entered the room and locked the door behind you. You just hadn't noticed?' Betty Blake queried.

'Well, my girl, you see I can vouch for this. Earlier, just before I entered the room in question, I used a clothes brush to dust off my coat. Mr Dunn assisted; no marks were then in evidence. The mirror did not lie, neither when I passed the counter or clerks at work did I hear one snigger when my back was turned. Mr Dunn assures me my coat was perfectly spotless before I entered the room with the cash box.'

'Perhaps my niece could see the room — accompanied by myself of course,' suggested Aunt Medley, Betty in full agreement, sipping her Earl Grey.

'Why, Miss Medley, after we have polished off this most delicious repast of tea and cakes we shall visit the bank at once. The City and Counties Bank should be honoured. Now, if I might draw your attention to the church bazaar of the 14th. The entrance fee I believe should be raised from a halfpenny to a penny. What as a committee member are your thoughts?'

The room proved exactly as described — functional. The windows barred, furniture consisting of the bank manager's desk and swivel chair, a small coffee table, a safe, a filing cabinet in one corner, the walls tastefully decorated by a number of water colours but most pertinently Betty Blake focused on a large Swiss cherry brown cuckoo clock carved with squirrels, birds and leaves. Tiny doors above a gold clock face displaying Roman numerals sprung open on the hour. The wall clock was hung directly behind where Mr Andrews normally leant over his desk, his back exposed, when dealing with everyday duties such as opening mail, signing letters concerned with clients' money.

While Aunt Medley and Mr Andrews were busy discussing church matters, Betty sidled over to where the cuckoo clock was placed, chains hooked with wooden dangling fir cones. It was nearly three o'clock and this proved fortuitous. 'Why, what a dull old tired cuckoo, the spring mechanism must have wound down,' exclaimed Aunt Medley, pausing from her conversation to listen, the bank manager paying little heed.

'Needs windin' s'pect,' said he.

Shooh, shooh, shooh, shooh, hoooooh — the mechanical cuckoo did sound decidedly flat and slow, not its usual chirpy self. But by now Betty, blessed with a real talent in observing almost insignificant details, had noticed a scrunched up ink pellet normally flicked in class by means of a rubber band at the person sat in front of you, or in the next row, hid over by the waste basket. The coffee table, she quickly realised, had been shifted across the carpet so someone of her height, perhaps a bit taller, could reach up and, by opening the little double doors, tamper with the cuckoo clock by winding the hour hand so a pellet could be ingenuously incorporated in the spring mechanism, the inky missile to be propelled exactly on the hour when the cuckoo sprang forth, from that angle easily able to strike the back of the bank manager's pristine light grey frock coat and splat it with ink while he worked at his desk, so that when Mr Andrews left the room, he should be open to ridicule.

Making sure the adults were not looking, the girl snatched the pellet off the carpet, placing it in her jacket pocket, no-one any the wiser, but she, Betty Blake, now had a good idea who was the mischief maker responsible.

★   ★   ★

'What a pity you could not solve the mystery of the locked room, Betty. Now that really is a puzzle worthy of your Sherlock by A.C. Doyle, but you're still only eleven, dear. Who knows, in time and with more experience under your belt . . . '

'Really,' said the girl, being passed a charity tin labelled 'Church Roof Restoration Fund', for she and her aunt intended to put in an hour or so collecting along the high street.

Deliberately taking her stance outside the City & Counties Bank, at five past five o'clock Betty was pleased to see young

Harry Ginn who was fourteen, short and stocky and recently left school to be a messenger employed in the bank's post room emerge from the building with a large grin on his face, peering into his just-opened weekly wage packet, his tongue practically lolling out.

'Don't ever do that again — it was horrid!' said the determined girl wagging her collecting tin under his nose, blocking the youth's path.

'What do you mean, Betty?'

'Cuckoo clocks.'

Harry went white and swallowed hard. She continued her onslaught. 'You work in the post room and as the messenger go in and out of the rooms delivering and collecting mail from desks. That gave you every opportunity to fiddle with the clock while Mr Andrews was out. His wife and the housekeeper must take ages removing the stupid ink spots from the bank manager's frock coat. Don't do it again, or else.'

Betty wagged the tin and Harry Ginn reluctantly fed two shiny new pennies through the money slot.

TWELVE YEARS OLD

The Old Pram Puzzle

The village to the English is a quaint place of quiet retreat with cricket on the green and church bells chiming over the duck pond. The dear old parish council, of which Aunt Medley was a staunch member, was responsible for conserving lamp posts, roadside verges and the village stocks, yet, as young Betty Blake was about to discover, beneath the slow paced rural veneer lie dark and wicked deeds committed by the *totally unsuspected*.

One bright, sunny morning during the school break Betty's Scottie dog, Bertie, slipped its leash, her white woolly pet scrabbling through a gap in the fence beside a farm track, a roughshod cinder and broken brick right of way used mostly by wagons, shire horses and the odd traction engine heading for Dale's farm.

Beyond the fence was a long, narrow garden. There was a summerhouse in poor repair, and an undulating lawn flanked by shrubbery led down a dip to a gabled house with steeply pitched roof and tall chimneys called 'Laburnums'. Mrs Prudence Felworth lived there with her husband, keeping herself to herself mostly, and was little seen about the village; very occasionally she attended church.

Minding her skirts, ducking through the hole in the fence, the little girl was drawn to the summerhouse, noticing, while calling for her dog, an old battered pram with a black tasselled hood parked close by under a small hardwood tree bearing clusters of yellow flowers, a laburnum, the seed pods of which were deadly poisonous according to her class teacher at the village school house, Miss Tern. The chromium rim of one of the rear spoked wheels was buckled out of true.

Curious, the girl peered into the pram. She could clearly see reels of cotton, ribbons and withered bunches of lucky heather, all mouldy due to rain having accumulated in the bottom creating stagnant water, so the black monstrosity had been parked here under the laburnum tree for some time. The pram most likely belonged to a gypsy, a lucky heather lady selling her wares about the village. There was a tinker encampment along Prudie Lane — where Mr Stumpy could be found.

The girl proceeded up the creaky steps of the summerhouse and, in the gloom, decided to sit on the bench for a while. The dog would seek her out soon enough. She could hear her Bertie scampering about in the undergrowth, getting his paws and woolly fur so very dirty.

When she twisted round she realised she was not alone. She had company, the *first human remains* she would ever encounter; in fact, a skeleton dressed in rags smothered by a clingy mass of cobwebs, a gossamer veil spun by spiders over time. The skeleton was knitting, needles positioned between calcified knuckle joints. Even in the poor light she could make out a discarded pattern book damply stuck to the floorboards. Parting the cobwebs, a skull grinned back at her, a short clay pipe clamped between its uneven yellow teeth.

Given this surprise at such a young age, Betty remained curious, detached. She thought methodically, like a coroner. There was no question of her being scared of a dead person and certainly not a skeleton.

To her obvious way of thinking the remains clearly belonged to a gypsy whose property was that old, tatty perambulator. A lucky heather lady who was very old passed away suddenly while smoking her pipe and knitting, putting her feet up for a bit. That represented the obvious way of thinking, the logical route. Parting the cobwebs further, she realised the skeleton was wearing a ring on its bony finger, a big gold one, a man's signet ring, the initials clearly 'C.F.'.

'What are you doing here?' Big bosomed Mrs Felworth, looking incredibly annoyed, came stomping up the steps brandishing her rubber-tipped cane, her long black clothes forbidding. 'You have no right to be here, child, this is my property, my garden.'

'I'm so sorry,' Betty replied, gathering her skirts, about to leave. 'Bertie ran through a hole in the fence you see, and . . . '

'Come here, dog!' Mrs Felworth boomed. All of a sudden the repentant woolly Scotch terrier made an appearance, cowering and whimpering in the presence of this formidable, nasty woman. The dog was covered in mud, of course, and would require a good bath. Betty sighed.

★   ★   ★

'Mother, Auntie, I wonder . . . when was the last time you saw Mr Felworth, Cecil . . . Mrs Felworth's husband about the village?' enquired Betty, helping herself to more salad lunch then in progress, Mrs Appleton, the Blake's servant hovering over proceedings, clacking her dentures audibly.

'About a year ago,' answered mother, gathering radishes onto her plate, 'before he went off to serve the empire as a colonial policeman in India. I saw him driving their dog cart; he waved.'

'Yes, I should say round about a year; I encountered Cecil in the bank,' added Aunt Medley. 'His wife told everyone at the village coffee morning of his sudden departure to Delhi. Duty, a want to serve his country in some capacity. I suppose Mrs Felworth of course couldn't bear the heat and dust out there and the lengthy sea voyage.'

'But he's not in India,' insisted Betty, 'he's up the road in the garden, well rotted down.'

'You must learn to keep these radical impressions of yours under check, my dear. Next, you'll be telling your mother and I he was murdered!' exclaimed Mrs Medley, smiling condescendingly, but then frowning.

'He *was* murdered! Oh, Auntie, I saw the shifty way that woman looked at that tree, the yellow flowering laburnum where the pram was shaded. Miss Tern at school told us the seed pods were dangerous. What if she mashed them down to a fine powder and put it in his cocoa?'

'Rather 'old hat', not very original. But I suppose your theory deserves some merit. What's all this about Mr Felworth being composted?'

'She killed him and made her husband up to look like a gypsy, a lucky heather lady knitting a sock or something, sat him in the summer house, let nature do the rest to fool the police. But, you see, she forgot to remove his gold signet ring engraved with the initials 'C.F.' which stand for Cecil Felworth, don't they? They must do.'

Goodnight Petunia

The week *after the funeral* Mr Sydmouth, the village solicitor, now a widower bereaved by the unfortunate passing of his dear wife in her sleep, was holding a sherry morning at his house opposite.

'The poor dear man,' Aunt Medley proposed, 'losing his wife so suddenly. How long have we known him, darling?'

'Simply ages,' answered Mrs Blake fussing over her daughter's beret. 'Mr Sydmouth, our legal man, knew you as a baby, Betty. He and his wife were present at your christening.'

'Goodness,' said Aunt Medley, glancing out of the window, a creaky farm wagon hauled by a shire horse clopping past. 'Just look at the time. We must hurry, Mr Sydmouth shall be expecting us. I've just seen Miss Todd and Mr Bissel, our verger, going in.' She allowed their long-time domestic servant, Mrs Appleton, to assist putting on her coat.

The sherry morning progressed in a dull way for Betty; she wished desperately to escape the constant adult babble. 'I shall just visit the upstairs closet, Mother.'

'Third door along the landing, you can't miss it, dear,' said mother, turning directly to speak with the vicar who was nibbling at a slice of seedcake.

Climbing the stairs, Betty reached the upstairs landing, the smell of wax polish and moth balls prevalent. The first door she came to was open; this must have been the bedroom where Mrs Sydmouth passed on; the bed was a hideous mahogany one, with a big strapping headboard. So it was in this bed Petunia Sydmouth, a not unattractive woman, had breathed her last. Betty was unable to resist having a peep around; the curtains were open, the room being aired.

She opened the door to the bedside cabinet. Inside on the bottom shelf a chamber pot, on the upper a folded towel and a drinking mug, yet to be taken down to the kitchen and rinsed. Betty thought the cocoa must have been poorly boiled in the pan for a queer fizzy sediment remained at the bottom of the mug.

Curiosity might have killed the cat, but it certainly didn't kill her when poking around upstairs. She paused before the mirror of an old mahogany dresser, tucking a stray curl into her beret, but what caught her eye more than her own appearance was a mark, a recent scorch burn ruining the varnished surface of the dresser where were gathered hair brushes, perfume bottles and assorted toiletries. She had seen an exact similar crescent-shaped burn on the bench in Mr James' glasshouse when Miss Tern and a group of children visited the walled kitchen garden up at the manor one afternoon.

Quitting the bedroom she nearly tripped over a pile of draught excluders, cloth worms put at the base of the doors each winter to keep out the cold. These had evidently been brought out of storage for they were still damp to the touch, covered in a fine mould.

★ ★ ★

The well-weathered old Georgian country house, 'The Beeches' where resided the lord of the manor, Sir Winton Clarke, whose youngest son, Alfred, featured very briefly in 'The Sweet Shop Murders' came into view as the pony-trap clopped round the bend, Betty's best friend Lizzie jogging the reins. The carriage rattled to a standstill opposite the head gardener's cottage set along a muddy lane, the glasshouses and walled kitchen garden serving Sir Winton's estate seen nearby.

'I shall not be long,' Betty said, jumping down, patting the pretty pony. 'Then we can go back to the village for ices and buns at the tea shop.' She blinked for it was a blue sky day and the summer sun severe.

The cottage belonged to the head gardener, but his wife came to the door wiping her hands on her pinafore. She possessed a red, gleaming, friendly face. 'Mr James be at lunch, my girl. What can I do for thee, child? Are you both after some bunches of violets? They beeze on sale at the gates.'

'No, I wanted to find out about a

crescent-shaped scorch burn on the bench of your melon house.'

'Bless thee, tha's a queer request for a little girl, but I knows to what you refer. We'll leave ole lummox to ee's lunch an' not bother 'im.' She thought for a bit. 'That burn mark comes from a spirit lamp what burns pure nicotine. The base gets ever so hot, see, an' being made o' metal, once the nicotine's boiling in its little cup above the flame can mark wood. I 'opes you b'aint about to light one yourself, deary, for them lamps is deadly poisonous to humans; used by Mr James for fumigatin', 'secticide for the glass-houses, like.'

★ ★ ★

'Oh, *a murder is announced* is it?' said Edwina Blake, doing the washing-up, waiting for her daughter to come and dry.

'I tell you, Petunia was murdered, Mummy. Mrs Sydmouth was sent to sleep by powders in her cocoa, and then Mr Sydmouth crept in and sealed the windows and the base of the door with

106

cloth worms brought in from storage in the garden shed; that's why they were damp to the touch. It's summer; you don't even need those thingies for keeping out draughts.'

'And liquid nicotine burnt off a spirit lamp filled the bedroom with noxious vapour. Where do you get these ideas from, Betty? I've mentioned before, keep that horrid imagination of yours in check. But you would make a first-rate mystery writer of detective stories, I'll give you that, say like Miss Oliphant or Miss Bradden.'

'Mr Sydmouth did it. It's a *sleeping murder*. Lizzie agrees, she'll back me up.'

'A first-class solicitor, my dear,' said Aunt Medley, 'a popular, well-liked member of my church, chairman of the parish council; sings in the choir. Now, for heaven's sake, enough of that Mr Sydmouth nonsense. Take this dishcloth and go and help your mother.'

Mr H.T. Sydmouth was indeed the chairman of the parish council upon which Aunt Medley often sat, but even chairpersons, those of an exemplary, impeccable character, can go badly wrong. Overseeing road repairs, organising rudimentary policing, sitting on sanitary and poor law boards, regular meetings with the vicar are not in themselves enough to stave off a calculated murder where the perpetrator believes themselves to have committed the so-called 'perfect crime' and to have got off scot free.

In fact, a murder *was* announced, for the *Lyminster Chronicle* ran an article a fortnight later. Apparently the solicitor hanged himself after admitting in a note he killed his wife in the manner described because she was carrying on with a young man in Wellingford. The police were of the view no third party was involved, so Betty was entirely vindicated.

Calling at Creesdale

'Beg pardon Mr Fraser, zir, but there's a corfin bound for Creesdale, I'll bring it up from the parcels office on the station trolley.'

Sat in the compartment at the back of a two coach train, Betty Blake could overhear the guard and porters as they made last minute preparations for departure at eleven o'clock. Her best friend Lizzie Meredith sat opposite on the cloth covered seat.

'Oh, Betty, we'll have such jolly fun at the department store, and lunch in the restaurant on the third floor.' The girls were jubilant on their day out.

'Got me the flower, fish and poultry boxes,' droned a man's voice. 'Bags of seed potatoes, mail sack and baskets of plums,' said the guard standing by to assist loading the elm coffin mostly covered in canvas presumably for protecting the wood finish. The branch did occasionally transport coffins along the line and it was normal. 'Not too 'eavy, zen.'

'Aye, not like the last one; some big fat bloke. Murder it were, nearly did me back in.'

Betty and Lizzie couldn't help giggling, poking their heads out of the compartment window. The stationary train was due out in five minutes. The sunny platform was alive with sparkling rainbow patterns, the station bedecked with colourful flower tubs, hanging baskets and window boxes, the smell of sooty smoke wafting down the train from the huffing locomotive up front.

'Right, that's that Mr Fraser, blow your whistle, wave the green flag and you're off, corfin stowed allus right.'

'No bother.'

Doors slammed, the engine tooted its whistle, echoing about the station precincts, and couplings clanked as the train moved steadily out of the country station.

The girls talked excitedly to one another. '*The four points* are these,' said Lizzie passing her bag of pineapple chunks, 'one . . . grandma Nibbs uses a witch hazel broomstick, two . . . she owns a big black cat, three . . . she makes potions up into bottles, four . . . she's ugly and has a hairy top lip and warts on her chin.'

'The grandmother absolutely hates the fat policeman. Golly, you know she may have cast another of those horrid spells, that's why he's getting all these bicycle punctures, flat tyres at the drop of a hat; the last one forced him to walk for miles between villages. My Aunt Medley thinks he needs a new bike, but we know different.'

Talk drifted to purchasing new bonnets, and the latest Miss Bradden pot boiler which they both liked lots. The rustic charm of a branch line station cannot be denied. At the next stop, Wormly Halt, the train rattled to a standstill.

The porter at these halts had plenty of time to darn his socks, cook meals and work on his flower and vegetable plots. Here, amid the twittering bird-song and gentle hissing of the engine, an interesting altercation took place. The guard was evidently sorely perplexed and had summoned the porter to his assistance.

'The coffin; I ain't travelling in the guard's van n'more with that thing,' he said, shakily. 'It's alive, summat's alive in there. I 'eard long fingernails scratching the underneath of the lid. Ghastly, the smell of decay is everywhere. Something that's alive, but not . . . '

'A *living dead*. I catch your drift, Mr Fraser. Did it bite you with its fangs? There's blood on yer shirt collar, man!'

'Naw, that were from cutting meself shaving. But, honestly Mr Tempest — sounded like long, calcified fingernails, blinkin' talons scratching against the lid. I'm fair petrified after travelling in the guard's van all alone. The dead has come alive, that coffin h'ain't right.'

By now, Betty and her friend Lizzie had got out of the compartment, stood in the sunshine listening to unfolding events.

'Best if we get young Lidden, my junior porter, to run into the village for a priest. Isn't that the correct procedure? *A vampire* is what we got 'ere, guvnor,' said the porter anxiously.

'Might I take a look? Only a peep,' asked Betty curiously, not very impressed by the lack of nerve.

'Wha', you, a girl?' exclaimed the guard.

'I might just be able to solve the puzzle. I'm rather good at that sort of thing, as Lizzie here will tell you.' Without asking permission, the girl clambered up into the van, fearless of 'the undead', more concerned to get to the heart of the matter. Vampires, she realised from basic reading of girls' adventure annuals only ever came out at night, after all.

Clues were forthcoming. When she pulled across the canvas sheet, she was amazed to spot tiny air holes bored into the elm lid. What's more, the lid was loosely held in place, hinged along one side. By now the porter joined her, helping to lift the lid. The waft of liquid manure, the pungent, acrid stench in the guards van was intense, providing a further clue.

As the lid creaked open, Betty and Mr Tempest were confronted by a dumpy black and tan sow resting lazily on its side on a soiled bed of straw. The pig snorted and belched before, unbothered, it went back to sleep, *five little pigs* nestling at its stomach teats.

'Well I never!' exclaimed the porter, scratching his beard. 'The village wheelwright, carpenter Joe Osmond at Lyminster, acts as the undertaker. He also part owns a smallholding out at Creesdale, a pig farm. This fellow must have utilised one of his spare coffins to transport the sow and her offspring. She were fed a mash of bottled beer and barley oats to keep her sedated for the railway journey up the line. I'll not write out a complaint chit on this occasion, but when I next see him at the Mitre Inn I'll be bound to have words. Carry on here, Mr Fraser, this girl is to be commended. Your name please, young lady?'

'Betty Blake.'

*   *   *

After shopping in town, making the return journey along the branch, the girls laden down with packages, strolled happily back to the village. The sun was still up and it was boiling hot. Along Old Pasture Lane they met the fat policeman looking very despondent; he was pushing a brand new bicycle, waddling along.

'It's no good,' he gasped, flushed red and sweating profusely. 'I'm still getting punctures, that's three today already. Why me, what have I done to deserve this?'

'Your bicycle clips. Take them off at once,' cried Betty, realising at last what others could not. 'You see, Mr Johns. What accompanies you when you're out riding?'

'Yes, by jingo, my cycle clips. I've worn these for years.'

The fat policeman, at Betty's specific direction, let her examine the inside of each springy metal ring. Strange symbols, *runes* they were called, magical diagrams had been scratched with the point of a sharp instrument, creating ill luck to the wearer. Grandma Nibbs had been responsible — she was sure of it.

Happy Valentine

'Oh Yeez knoweth hows I got sech a gift, Miss Medley. I'm eighty-six come June. I done got a box o' Rowntrees plain assortment from an admirer; must be an admirer, eh, what thought so kindly to place 'em on my step as a surprise for Valentine's Day. Who be my Prince Charming? Ol' Mr Smith, ol' Pennywhistle, my ol' flame bedridden, ninety-year-ol' Sedge Carter, or praps tis a young whelp wants to favour me for my savings. I'll knowest soon enough. Yeez canna keep a secret in our village fer long.'

The elderly widow, Mrs Lugg, her lardy plump face aglow, her many chins wobbling, departed in what was for her high spirits, her surprise Valentine chocolates a point of mystery. Young Betty Blake, accompanying her spritely aunt, continued along Old Pasture Lane to the shops, remarkably accosted by yet another old lady, this time a cadaverous spinster, Miss Egrams, outside the butcher's.

'Boxa chocolates on me winda sill; Rowntrees. Me of all folk. Some fella's wishful Valentine. Yuzz neffer believe what men's fancies are these days, Miss Medley,' she sighed. 'I'm still only seventy-six, mind, I haff a bit put by. Oh yuzz, I can still turn a bloke's 'ead at the Mitre alrigh'.

'Were these Rowntrees chocolates plain or milk? enquired the girl primly.

'Allus plain, Miss Betty.'

Like her aunt, Betty Blake was intrigued by this spate of Valentine gifts in the village. Such generosity on the part of romantically inclined men . . . or was it?

'Couple of layer. Oh, I'll enjoy 'em,' she enthused, 'although who I wonder seeks me out as his special love, choosing to bestow this mark of affection? Mind thee, I 'ear Jeb Crane, that smelly old labourer wha' lives in the tithe cottage got a box of similar dropped in his bird bath.'

The next port of call was the village sweet shop further along owned and run

117

by Mrs Staple. 'Can't understand it, Miss Medley,' she said dully, stretching up for a glass stoppered jar of mints on the shelf beside identical jars of fruit gums, humbugs and pineapple chunks temptingly displayed. 'My stock's down, see. Half dozen chocolate selections kep' in a cardboard box stacked round the back of the counter. Where can'st they be? Musta mislaid 'em, reckon. But enough of that. Haven't seen yer for a bit, Miss Medley. 'Ere, step round the back, time for a chinwag, an' I'll make us a nice pot o' tea. I'm gasping, been on the go since half pass five I 'ave.'

'But Mrs Staple,' pointed out the girl. 'Is it wise to leave the sweet counter unattended? You're still showing an 'OPEN' sign on the shop door, aren't you?'

'Neffer you mind, gal. The shop bell allus rings when there's a customer. No bother.'

So, obviously the Valentine's Day chocolates were stolen goods pilfered from the sweet shop . . . but how?

Aunt Medley helped the slow-witted

shopkeeper boil the kettle and spooned leaves into the teapot. The biscuit barrel was placed on the table and they all settled down.

Betty quickly put her brains to good use. 'On any day last week, were you perchance called away, left the shop unattended, Mrs Staple?' asked the girl, looking very serious.

'My dear,' cautioned Aunt Medley, sensing her charge's lack of tact. 'Do be a trifle less impertinent, stop trying to ape that new Sherlock Holmes character in the Beeton's annual you do so like to read. Shall we dispense with the coroner's summing up for now? Leave that sort of thing to P.C. Johns at the police house.'

But far from being offended, Mrs Staple remembered she had left the shop unattended. 'Now you'se mention it, young Betty, I 'eard a bang out back, see, that made me start, nearly jump out of my skin so'se I left my place at the counter and came straight back here to my parlour. I wuzz surprised fert the amount of smoke in the room, but of course I knew all along it were the coal.

That blinkin' coal's poor quality. I ain't ordering n'more from Mr Heath agin; I wants proper Welsh coal from the merchant at the railway yard in future.'

Sipping her tea while the adults chatted on other general topics, Betty already had formed a clear theory as to how 'the chocolate robbery' took place. How it was done, that is, not 'whodun-nit'. That would require further clues, but the fact boys were involved, a banger thrown into the coal fire in the parlour at the rear of the house to distract Mrs Staple, cause her to leave the shop temporarily, was a useful lead to follow. She saw it all pretty clearly. One of a pair of youths must have wedged the shop door so the bell didn't automatically ping-ping-a-ling when opened from the street. It was he who must have also entered the shop at the given opportunity when Mrs Staple hurried out back as the loud bang of the firework occurred. The first youth sidled round the unattended counter, swiping boxes of Rowntrees chocolates, each manufactur-er's carton containing a half dozen chocolate assortments.

The second boy had previously sneaked over the garden wall from the back of the house and by visiting the unlatched kitchen door had entered Mrs Staple's parlour, hurling the banger into the coal fire as arranged, causing it to explode, before running off. The juvenile crime was clearly premeditated, coordinated, that much was certain.

★ ★ ★

That evening, using her initiative when she was taking her dog for a walk, Betty managed to cleverly retrieve an empty Rowntrees confection box out of the dustbin belonging to old Mrs Lugg who lived in one of a group of thatched timber and wattle cottages. The elderly recipient of a Valentine's day gift, she had certainly indulged her sweet tooth, polishing off the lot. A couple of incriminating clues were immediately apparent: (a) sticky fingers consistent with the residue from a twisty stick of barley sugar, the girl's fingertips adhering revoltingly to the tacky smudge marks on the box and (b) clear perforations visible, creasing and slightly denting the lid.

★ ★ ★

Ginger Cade was clearly surprised to see his fellow pupil at school turn up at the farmhouse so unexpectedly. His father tilled the soil, milked cows and was a sheep farmer and leased his working farm from the lord of the manor, Sir Winton Clarke. The freckle-faced boy, a carrot top if ever, peered suspiciously from beneath the porch lantern, his big rubbery lips parted revealing uneven, decayed teeth.

'What d'ya want, Blake? Me an' me bruvver's busy, can't it wait?'

'Ginger, you always have a bag of barley sugar in your desk. You have a keen liking for twists of the stuff.'

'Aye, so wot?'

'You love twists of barley sugar.'

'Yeah, Blake, I does. Free worl' ain't it, wot sweets we eat.'

Her Scottie dog barked, yapping, and

from within the house came a happy barking in response. A beautiful collie bounded to the door, a top sheep dog, fun loving of noble breeding. Sheep, when counted, are made to run between two hurdles, or gates, in pairs, which Bridget the collie did very well and for which she won many first prize rosettes.

The girl stooped down and made a fuss; both pets got on well and tails were joyously wagging. 'Tell me what happened, Ginger,' she asked, fondling the collie's ears, glancing up. 'You and your brother stole those chocolates from the village sweet shop, brought them back to the farm. What next, Bridget?' she cooed. 'You tell me; you know, don't you, sweetie?'

'Dunno. Honest, I dunno. Oh, alrigh', Betty, I can see it's no use. I'd better come clean. Promise me you won't tell on us to P.C. Johns. Please swear on God's honour.'

'Promise.' The boy seemed convinced enough.

'Well, for starters, me an' me bruvver neffer ate one of them Rowntrees, nor got

a chance to sell 'em on, because my dog
'ere nicked 'em all from the barn durin'
the night and I dunno where they went.'

The Seven Suet Balls

In winter blackbirds and robins are very partial to currant cake, sultanas and biscuit crumbs. Blue and great tits, of which there are many, like plenty of peanuts. Now that the weather had turned iron cold and January snow lay thick on the ground, to supplement the strung up bacon rind, Betty took up to the bird table some stale bread and cake crumbs, sometimes quite reticent pairs of birds, like nuthatch and bullfinches, proving a delight to watch from the kitchen window.

Also, a favourite was bird feed balls made from suet. Aunt Medley and mother preferred them readymade, regularly purchasing a quantity from Miss Caterham, a member of the church committee and engaged to be married to the vicar, who always used the best ingredients, and indeed in summer sold eggs, damsons and gooseberries from outside her garden gate placed on a little three-legged stool with a jam jar for putting money in. The bird balls were so popular the ironmonger and the fruiterer in Lyminster High Street put them on sale.

The girl hesitated, brushing scraps onto the bird table from her plate. She had noticed the bird ball had been torn from its hook and was lying some distance away beneath a tree in pieces, spread out on the snow.

Crossing over the white patch of speckled lawn she pondered the ground. The suet ball had definitely been ripped apart, not merely pecked. It had only just been hung up the evening before. Peering over the wall it was obvious the neighbour's suet ball had suffered a similar fate. Was a big crow, or a fox, or stoat responsible? But no, interestingly, Betty was quick to grasp a person had been here, a person intrigued enough to use a lamp to see by, for the round metal base had left an imprint in the snow crust and also a pair of wellington boots, for a number of deep, plodding footprints existed, although someone had tried to brush them out with a branch, a clumsy attempt, failing to do this properly. The birds, of course, didn't mind, happily fluttering about pecking at the morsels.

Before it started snowing again, out of curiosity, more of an exercise, Betty went back to the cottage and returned up the garden five minutes later with her school ruler and a notepad and pencil bag. She knelt down and carefully recorded the measurements of the only decent remaining chunky-soled wellington boot print. After this, knotting another suet feed ball on its hook on the bird table, she went back to seek the warmth of the kitchen, showing Aunt Medley her accurate sketches, with which she was very pleased.

★   ★   ★

At a quarter past twelve, there came an urgent knock at the back door. With steaming lunchtime saucepans atremble on the range, mother wiping her hands on a cloth hurried to open the door, to be greeted by a hulking great moon-faced simpleton of over fifty who barged in like a bull in a china shop, her forlorn, miserable expression saying much.

'Sorry, Mrs Blake,' she sobbed. 'Betty, I'm done fer. Dunno, dunno how — nuffink I done. Wuzz earrinks pinched, see, frum Missie Caterham's place.'

'Earwigs?'

'Earwinks.'

'Oh.'

It transpired large-limbed Mary Chaff with her short-cut, ginger hair, the dim giantess who always wore shepherds' smocks and sandals whatever the weather, having the unfortunate tendency to happen to be in the wrong place at the wrong time had been accused of stealing jewellery again. She was, embarrassingly, in full public view, chased down the road by P.C. Johns the fat policeman, utilising his brand new bicycle to mount the pavement and apprehend the child-woman on account of a pair of valuable antique ruby earrings, an engagement present from the padre to his future intended, stolen from the kitchen window sill, the property of Miss Ann Caterham who resided in a bungalow on the corner.

When cautioned, Mary felt so humiliated, unsure of herself she started to become muddled, make silly excuses, started to look more and more red-faced, guilty of the crime befitting the role of a burglar.

Later at the police house her elderly mother gave a good account of her frumpy daughter and, being fair minded, P.C. Johns did not, at that stage, press charges. However, the problem remained; Mary Chaff had visited Miss Caterham's bungalow that day to collect a box of half dozen hens' eggs, remaining for a mug of tea in the kitchen, so she was still a main suspect. If proved guilty, the matter should have to go before the local Justice of the Peace, Sir Winton Clarke, a great personage and chief landowner in the area.

The cosy range, the homely scene in the Blake's kitchen with the aroma of baked 'toad in the hole' and crusty apple tart wafting temptingly from the oven, had the positive effect of calming down

Mary, as did the prospect of lunch, to which mother invited her, laying out a fourth place mat on the starched table linen and drawing up the largest of the cottage chairs.

'Bird balls,' said Betty, thoughtfully.

'Bird balls? Why are you all of a sudden so concerned with bird balls?' queried Mrs Blake, spooning out cabbage, somewhat mystified. The girl knew that Miss Denton, and Mrs Bunn next door, regularly placed pre-paid orders with the greengrocer. Mrs Denton always ordered seven at a time for feeding the birds in her garden and this got the clever girl thinking . . .

★   ★   ★

Peggy Denton, a spritely lady, lived at Old Postman's Cottage opposite, an ancient flint and brick granary. She employed two servants, Mr Stepney, the gardener, who lived in Lyminster and bicycled to work, and Mrs Chard, who came in daily to help with the housework. The old lady was delighted to have company, especially that of young Betty Blake whose aunt she sat beside in church. The wee cottage, like the granary, a landmark in the village, was approached by a straight path brushed and cindered with coal fire ash.

The cottage, formerly owned by a postman, was built in brick and white clapboard with a roof of well-weathered clay tiles. Betty was cordially shown into the spacious living room by the servant, daft Mary, the well-known simpleton of Lyminster was required to remain outside on the front porch, the snow starting to fall again. Betty did her best to explain.

'What?' Miss Denton was absolutely dumb-founded, amazed at the girl's consequent request, 'all seven of them? But I only received my order from the shop a day or so back. Mrs Chard hasn't even strung one up on my bird table from this new batch yet.'

'This is really, really important,' emphasised Betty Blake, daft Mary stood outside shuffling her bare, sandalled feet on the welcome mat, the top of her head capped by snow.

'All seven?'

131

'Yes, please.'

Reluctantly, the lady fetched the brown paper bag containing her order from the greengrocer, allowing each bird ball in turn to be prised apart and crumbled between deft fingers on a sheet of newspaper. Thereafter, to everyone's surprise, was found an exquisite pair of ruby earrings, which, after a good douse under the tap, gleamed like new.

★   ★   ★

Mary Chaff and Betty turned up unexpectedly at the bungalow in Falcon Road just round the corner. The lovely antique silver and ruby earrings, a present from the vicar to his beloved, received with coos of delight from Miss Caterham, who, although wary of the big, strapping woman-child, could not have been happier.

On a more serious note, however, Betty brought out her writing pad and spread out a page of her accurate drawings of the dimensions of the wellington boot print found in her garden that morning near the bird table and explained in detail the vandalism of the suet balls. This provoked everyone to stare accusingly at a dainty pair of wellingtons put next to Miss Caterham's larger galoshes on the tiles over by the broom cupboard. A maid, a young girl who had been rinsing glasses over by the sink, let out an anguished howl. She collapsed in a chair sobbing, confessing to everything. 'Please, please, P.C. Johns must not know,' or she'd be in for it from her pa.

Miss Caterham demanded an explanation. With not much prompting, Junipa, the maid, admitted snatching the valuable antique earrings off the sill and in a moment of stupidity, forming a crime in her mind, dropping them into the large bowl of suet on the kitchen table, a usual mixture of nuts, seeds and dried fruit, swilling it round with a wooden spoon so that the expensive earrings remained completely submerged in suet. Placing a dish cloth over the bowl she returned later to make up the bird feed balls, lining twenty of them on a tray.

By feeling around she knew exactly

which two balls would for certain contain the hidden earrings, having made sure the dollops of suet mixture she was moulding, patting into shape with her fingers had the earrings inside. Everything went without a hitch (Junipa was intending to purchase two of the bird balls for herself before she went home). Miss Caterham suspected not her, but daft Mary Chaff who had called at the bungalow for a box of eggs, of pinching her earrings off the sill, but then wretched Mrs Dovedale spoiled it all when she called unexpectedly, ruining the plan. She used the back door, snatched the tray and left some money in a china saucer on the kitchen dresser.

In the time it took Junipa to serve afternoon tea for the vicar and Miss Caterham in the next room, the plate of scones, fancy sandwiches and pot of Earl Grey tea, Mrs Dovedale the greengrocer's wife had nipped in and out, and the bird balls were gone. But she realised there was still hope of retrieving the precious earrings for on the kitchen dresser was left a list, including prepaid orders for the latest batch of twenty suet balls from: Mrs Bunn (5p.p.), Miss Denton (7p.p.), Mrs Blake (4p.p.), for sale four extra which were despatched, so the maid noted all this down in her memory, but by the time she got to the shop all the bird feed balls had been sold, so she began a desperate and futile search of gardens — all to no avail.

It was clear the maid's vanity, her wish to possess a fine pair of very beautiful and expensive earrings, left her infatuated, unable to resist the allure of twinkling rubies on the window sill. She had thus acted on impulse, rashly, and would — and did — receive a sound ticking-off.

The Clever Dog

'Oh, t'was a lovely occasion,' enthused Aunt Medley, shelling peas under the shade of an ash tree surrounded by colourful herbaceous borders in the sunny garden. Betty knelt beside her on the lawn cradling an enormous bowl full of shredded pods, oblivious to a couple of wasps buzzing inquisitively about her straw bonnet — about to settle.

Her aunt was not slow to act; she shooed them off with a folded *Times* newspaper, but wasps are tenacious and for some reason Betty had attracted the insects and they would soon be back.

'A stout oaken coffin, you see. The handles cleverly carved in the shape of doggie's paws, wonderful, and even a brass name plate screwed to the lid. Old Beezer, bless his cotton socks, certainly received a terrific send off. The dog was buried at the back of the garden by the holly hedge.'

'What was he exactly, Auntie? He was very big, bigger than most dogs I've ever seen in the village.'

Aunt Medley paused at her task, smiling at the memory. 'Beezer is what is commonly referred to as a cross, Betty — that is, between a Labrador and a Newfoundland. That gave him his strength and that build; tall as a man when stood on his legs, but the temperament — oh, the sweetest, gentlest, kindest nature. Children like yourself, my dear, simply adored him whenever he was desirous of trotting into the village from his kennel at Railway Cottage to see everybody and woof hello.'

'Mr Cribbins is a carpenter? A wood worker?'

'Yes, dear, rather a splendid one. Your doll's house was built by him, but his day job is in charge of the signal box on the Wellingford branch. I'm sure he will miss poor old Beezer for company in his cabin. Drat those beastly wasps. We'd better hurry indoors. Another three of them, that's five. The nest must be nearby. We don't want to get stung and our faces to swell. Wasps have vicious stings; bumble bees are alright in the garden, but not those things. I shall contact Mr Fuller.'

Betty and her aunt joined mother in the cool of the spacious drawing room upon a comfy sofa before a large brick settle, the fireplace hung with various horse brasses, decorative bellows and fire tongs. An inlaid cabinet stood beneath the window atop of which a porcelain milkmaid, vase of flowers and a very big bowl for fruit presided. To one side of the fireplace was a wrought iron lamp standard, and a brass vase sufficed for umbrellas over by the stable style front door.

'Wasps,' Aunt Medley reminded everyone, ordering tea from their domestic, Mrs Appleton, 'on the attack, ready to sting.'

'Oh dear, that is a nuisance,' said mother, glancing up from her crochet. 'I expect there's a nest in the orchard that needs smoking out. Mr Fuller is our man. Betty, would you help Mrs Appleton with the tea things, darling, there's a good girl.'

Betty and Aunt Medley were coming out of the pharmacist along the village High Street, only to bump into Mr Cribbins who had been delivering a number of his wooden flower tub creations to Faringdon's, the local ironmonger; the High Street retailer could not sell them quickly enough. The decorative windmill and wheelbarrow tubs proving so popular.

'Why, bless 'ee. Miss Medley, an' you too young Betty. Yer liked the doggie fooneral, eh ma'am?'

'Very fitting,' replied the aunt. 'The vicar spoke so eloquently, such a lovely sunny morning. Do you miss Beezer? Of course you must.'

'Allus I does ma'am, but the ol' boy 'oweffer poplar wi' folk, wuzz very ancient boned and arfritick, so it were for the best however 'ee . . . erm . . . '

The signalman paused in mid-sentence licking his lips, a glazed look in his eyes.

'Do go on Mr Cribbins.'

'I don't knows I should ma'am, butta . . . '

139

'Do stop procrastinating, out with it, man!' exclaimed Aunt Medley, putting down her shopping bag, a reassuring smile enough to prompt a response.

'I seen 'im these three times, Miss Medley. T'were getting dark, see, twilight, like as not. Luss evening I wuzz waterin' the borders in the garden at my cottage, thinking 'bout my supper; I 'ad a nice stew and dumplins' planned, then I 'ears barking familiar t'me over by the 'olly 'edge. Fer a flash there be me dear old dog jest as afore, waggin' 'is tail, tongue 'anging out. Jest normal like, but 'e weren't normal wuzz 'e — couldna been.'

★   ★   ★

Mr Cribbins had managed the same signal box all his working life; although paid less than his main line counterpart with many fewer trains, he often earnt pocket money repairing bicycles, rabbiting, building little garden windmills and flower tub wheelbarrows, and generally putting his woodworking skills to good use between trains. He had a responsible

140

job and must keep his eye on the signal, the instruments in his cabin and the crossing gates. Old Beezer had been well known to railway men on the line and his large wolfish presence at the station should be missed by passengers, for he quite freely roamed the platform and waiting rooms and was appreciated. Now he had a little crafted wood cross up by the holly hedge.

★ ★ ★

Young Miss Blake and her companion, Lizzie Meredith, bumped into their friends Snark Davis and Basil Thyme at the school gates. Snark, the undisputed conker champion, was a bit of a swot who, when he grew up, had no desire to become an engine driver, but wanted to join the library service and one day become custodian of Lyminster public library. Basil was the undisputed king of swots who came first in class at everything.

They went for tea and an iced bun at the teashop, Betty taking the lead suggesting that they take up the strange matter of the undead dog.

'Betty,' said Basil, 'you were brilliant in that seven suet balls business, in which you solved a mystery, but what puzzle draws you into this dog haunting nonsense? Clearly Mr Cribbins is off his top, a bit of a looney, wouldn't you agree?'

'I would,' said Snark, confidently.

'So would I,' agreed Lizzie.

'But it *is* a puzzler, don't you see?' insisted the young girl vehemently.

'That's just it, with this ghost wot-not,' continued Basil. 'I mean, suppose after Beezer died and was buried, Mr Cribbins, in his imagination, willed him back but not really; I mean, the dog don't sound that ghostly. I'd expect *the hound of death* to be absolutely RABID, red-eyed, snarling, fangs dripping blood.'

★　★　★

'Well, I must say, yorn a 'sceptical spectacles', ain't yer, Basil? I didna imagine nuffink; tell ya what, I dare you

142

children to stay in the garden when it starts to git dark, an' see fer yerselves I aint fibbing,' insisted Mr Cribbins, puffing on his pipe.

The signalman checked the special railway time clock above the mantelshelf in his cabin surrounded by his telegraph machines and the polished row of levers he pulled with a cloth to change the signals. Everyone was drinking tea out of chipped mugs. A bell pinged, a train was due. The fun of being so close to the railway track and to see a steam train approach was exciting and engrossing for the boys Snark Davis and Basil Thyme, but Betty was far more concerned about the ghost dog puzzle.

'I'm going to Mr Cribbins' garden. Coming Lizzie?'

'Alright.'

The girls climbed back down the signal box steps to the cinder path and made their way along beside the tracks to Railway Cottage where the signalman lived. A train whistle hooted in the distance round the curve.

'But why,' thought Betty to herself,

'why does the ever faithful Beezer show himself like this — return from the grave? Not to scare anyone it seems.'

The first clue was provided when Betty happened to notice an oxidised green coin nestling in the shorn tufts of grass just past the vegetable plot. Suddenly, a loud barking started up from behind the nearby holly hedge, making the girls jump, nearly scream and run for their lives. Could it be Beezer, the ghostly giant dog, the hound of death? Dr Lent, the village G.P., appeared wearing his tweed cap and plus-fours and shiny brown brogues. A tiny bundle of fur scampered from behind the hedge; it was a Chihuahua. What a loud and raucous bark it had for such a small animal. Quite unnerving, in fact, but the barking certainly didn't belong to Beezer, the ghost dog haunting the garden at Railway Cottage.

'Hello Betty Blake, and you Lizzie,' apologised the local medical practitioner scooping up his little dog. 'Queenie was very naughty and ran off the woodland footpath, got under the fence of Mr

Cribbins' garden, but I've got her now. Good evening to you both.' He doffed his cap and returned into the woods, crashing through the undergrowth, beating it back with his stout ash stick until he attained the fence just as a train further down went chuffing past the cottage into the station proper.

★ ★ ★

The girls came hurrying back up the timber steps to the signal box. Mr Cribbins was smoking his pipe, brewing more tea in the pot. The boys were playing Snap at the table. 'Mr Cribbins, Mr Cribbins!' Betty gasped, bursting into the cabin, her face flushed, all blotchy. 'Beezer wanted you to look at the holly hedge, to dig it up. That's why he came back as a ghost. Honestly, I found these old coins scattered under the bush, amongst the roots, six of them, a treasure trove!'

The signalman considered one of the coins in the palm of his grubby hand. 'Aye, s'pose so. Alrigh' Betty, I'll pop over between trains an' fetch me spade and pitchfork. The boys'll 'elp. I need a bit o' rope to drag that hedge outta ground, tug o'war like as not.'

Thus, to the children's delight, was discovered that evening at twilight a veritable hoard of gold: Roman coins, necklets and goblets tracing back to Pagan times, so Beezer's ghost was responsible for Mr Cribbins being in pocket to the tune of one hundred pounds when the Roman treasure was later sold to the British Museum by Mr Smith, a local historian and stalwart member of the Lyminster Archaeological Society.

The Moving Cushion

Old Pasture Lane, where young Betty Blake lived, was not normally known for its notoriety else morbid excitements. The lane was a rural retreat, a collection of pretty thatched and timbered cottages, a part of the tranquil English village scene, an agricultural community overseen by Sir Winton Clarke, lord of the manor.

However, upon a rainy, storm-clouded day in March, for the first time anyone could remember, Wellingford police, in the guise of Detective Crumpton and a number of officers and a sergeant, were summoned by P.C. Johns at the police house to attend a scene regarded as 'suspicious'.

Mrs Rutherford, a portly, spiteful old woman known to be penny pinching and something of a martinet by her neighbours, openly despised by her long suffering serving housekeeper, *Miss Hickson*, a woman in her late forties, a domestic, was discovered sat bolt upright in her winged armchair, staring ahead, a look of utter terror emblazoned on her pasty, lardy features.

'Quite dead' she was pronounced as such officially by the police surgeon in attendance, Dr Godfrey.

A horse ambulance and two hansoms were parked outside the cottage when Betty arrived back from school. The girl, curious to find out more, hurried down to the end of her garden and, climbing a pear tree in the orchard, was able to listen in to a confidential conversation taking place three gardens away between a detective and the fat policeman, Mr Johns.

'Miss Hickson, the servant woman, I believe is our protagonist. I intend to question her further tomorrow morning.'

'Her, certainly, or an intruder, say. The burden of evidence points this way. That old pussy, that old cat, Mrs Rutherford, widely known in the village as a gossip, had a dicky heart. We suppose she was deliberately, callously shocked to death. Dr Godfrey attested to this. He is yet to perform an autopsy and shall do so later at Wellingford.'

'Dear Lor', the look on that poor old spinster's face . . . ghastly!' remembered Inspector Crumpton, frowning.

'Awful.'

'Horrible business, horrible,' concluded the other.

By six o'clock, the police and the horse ambulance had departed, Old Pasture Lane returning to normal after the excitements. Betty ran round to the late Mrs Rutherford's cottage. Miss Hickson, the domestic, was still tidying up in the parlour before going home.

'Oh, how I hated that blinkin' woman,' she moaned, 'I really did. Only last week, the old battle-axe told me that after all my years of drudgery I was to receive ten shillings in her will, much of her savings being donated to an African missionary society.' She sniffed indignantly while Betty put the kettle on the hob of the range to boil water for tea.

'Lor, lumme, I never did kill her, you know. Oh, it was common knowledge we didn't get on, but murder! No, I'm just not inclined to that sort of thing. An intruder is the real culprit. Someone got in here last night when I left and did for her, although who was responsible I've just no idea.'

'But Mrs Rutherford was shocked by something.'

'*Someone*, you mean, yes, most assuredly dear.'

What caught the girl's eye was a loose cushion oddly out of place, left on the tiles of the back step. She picked it up. Damp, and then she sniffed the coarse material. Suddenly she was possessed of a brilliant idea. No policeman in the land would have taken her seriously and yet — what if Mrs Rutherford's *nemesis* was in fact . . .

Leaving Miss Hickson to brew the tea, Betty hurried next door to Mr Marshall's at No. 16. Returning but five minutes later, her face flushed with excitement, she endeavoured to explain to the domestic over a cup of tea what really happened to Mrs Rutherford. How she met her end.

'It happened like this, it really did,' said

Betty Blake, helping herself to a digestive from the biscuit barrel. 'Mrs Rutherford was sat, as agreed, in her usual favourite armchair before the fireplace, when surprisingly one of the embroidered cushions made of a stiff twill fabric with corner tassels walked off the sofa all by itself and then proceeded to walk by the kitchen to the back door which had been left ajar for the cat. This is what shocked the old lady so.'

'A moving cushion? Ridiculous, don't be so flippant, child. I may yet have to attend Wellingford police station tomorrow morning; that clever clogs Inspector Crumpton has it in for me.'

'You see, it was A LOBSTER, Miss Hickson and lobsters are quite happy to keep perfectly still, like under a rock along the seashore, until it decided to explore again. They can live on land for a bit as well as the sea, you know. Mr Marshall next door says so.'

'Well, I'll be blowed. How old are you, Betty?'

'Nearly twelve.'

'Alright, suppose your walking cushion

has possibilities; what does Mr Marshall have to do with all this, dear?' asked Miss Hickson, gingerly.

'That's the simple bit. The damp cushion on the back step smelt of salty seawater, a bit like at a stall that sells whelks and mussels, along by the harbour. Mother told me Mr Marshall is very partial to his seafood and only likes the freshest caught, which he buys off a local fisherman. You see, one of his lobsters he was going to boil alive to cook for his dinner escaped from its bath tub; he keeps them in the bath in plenty of water so they're really, really fresh.'

Mr Cribbins' Garden

'Mother's very pleased with her pair of wheelbarrow flower tubs, very much so,' mentioned Betty upon clambering up the steep signal box steps, entering Mr Cribbins' cabin closely followed by her chum, Snark Davis, keenly looking over her shoulder. 'Mama filled the tubs with pigsty manure and she and I shall plant polyanthus and geraniums'.

'Well, Miss Blake, I've got orders flooding in; me wheelbarra tubs is in five shops. Ironmongers keep' goin' on, but I ain't inclined to go into manufactory in a big way, I'd 'ave to start employing folk. I likes me bit o' carpentry, but loves the job on the railways more. Anyhow, Snarky, what's this I 'ear abart you wantin' to be a blinkin' librarian? Sissy woman's work h'aint it?'

Slumped in an ill-sprung chair before the coal fire crackling in the grate, above which was a little chimney piece, young

Davis refused to be drawn. So what if he did not fancy becoming an engine driver like his class mates? What of it?

'Course, if you wanna be an engine driver, it's a steep apprenticeship, starting as a loco cleaner, progressin' to footplate fireman. The GN&SR has a long waitin' list of applicants, priority given to sons or other close relations of railwaymen. But, when yer older, I'se could put in a good word for yer if yer like.'

'Ta all the same, Mr Cribbins, but I want to be a librarian.' Mind you, the lad had to admit he got a thrill when up here in the signal box; watching the trains brought a special joy as they rattled past on their way to Churley Tunnel, the huffing, puffing locomotives making all that loud din, the flames from the firebox visible from the cab, the shrill whistle of the engine as it issued wreaths of white smoke.

'Naw, I'm a GN&SR man through and through, a job for life. They employ me, see, and I will work this country box till retirement. I'm not paid so well as my main-line colleagues, mind, but I've fewer trains to handle, more spare time for rabbiting, mending bicycles, tending me flowers and veggies, making me wheelbarra tubs between services. Oh, it's a good life alrigh' . . . and a railway cottage 'n garden thrown in.'

'Your garden where your dear old Newfoundland Beezer is buried,' Betty reminded him.

'Up by the 'olly 'edge where we found all them Roman coins an wot-not, aye. I do miss the old fella, of course I does Betty, but I'll neffer replace 'im. Mind you, lately at dusk . . . ' A bell rang, interrupting the flow of his talk. Mr Cribbins looked sharp, snatching a rag and nimbly advancing to the row of levers. 'That'll be the up passenger service just left the station,' said he. Full of anticipation, Betty Blake and the boy sprang across to the signal box window overlooking the double set of tracks.

Later, sipping strong tea from chipped enamel mugs poured from a faithful brown teapot that rested on the table next to a plate of now much depleted goosebeny jam sandwiches and a basket of plums, Mr Cribbins, sitting back in his creaky, worn armchair, lit his pipe, savouring the rich aroma of tobacco filling the cabin.

The signal box was his responsibility, his domain — spotlessly clean, levers daily polished, the pinging electronic telegraph machine always listened out for, the signals and instruments a priority. One lapse of memory even on a country branch line could spell disaster; say a tunnel collision, a goods derailment. The gated level crossing must also be operated. Lately, he had seen many more cyclists, a newfangled contraption called a steam car and a small number of motors, but out here in the countryside, a rural, farming community, who needed motors? Horses were perfectly sufficient. You only had to see the shires, cart horses in everyday use hauling ploughs, wagonettes, delivery carts, yellow-wheeled dog carts, farmers' gigs and buggies harnessed to dappled mares and ponies to realise equines ruled! The branch railway rightly expected to shift produce and the local populace from one place to another; even coffins on occasions.

The signalman re-lit his pipe reflecting sentimentally, lost on another topic. 'Funny, I see'd my ol' dog bein' walked the other evening by the previous signalman's wife, Flora Abingdon, walking the dog through my garden at sundown along by my fruit trees.'

'Hold on a mo', your dog Beezer's dead, isn't he, sir?' queried Snark Davis, wondering if he'd heard right, all the while eyeing the basket of juicy plums.

Mr Cribbins nodded. 'Aye, as is old Flora Abingdon, dead an' gorn these past twenty year. But I see'd 'em boaf. Light startin' to fade, last Tuesday eventide. Funny 'ow ghosts appear when yer least expect 'em.'

'Were you perhaps mistaken?' asked Betty boldly, not wishing to call his memory of events into question, but doubtful all the same. 'Imagined it?'

'Nope, I see'd 'em fair 'n square, Betty. But that ain't the only thing I see'd, naw, it h'aint. Finish yer tea, there's something in the garden I wanna show you.'

With plenty of time between trains, no

passenger service or goods expected this hour of the day, the sun beating down, shining resplendently in the deep blue of the sky, Mr Cribbins led the children across to his cottage, thence round by the gate. The village railwayman's garden was much admired locally, passengers prone to peer out of the carriage windows as the stopping service clattered along beside the post and wire fence, clay pots of geraniums on the sun-drenched patio, the upper and lower ponds, the vast array of flowers in bloom, quirky, witty garden ornaments, the waterfall, the stream, the reed beds, the honeysuckle clematis arch, a water wheel, medieval style bridge built by Mr Cribbins of stout oak, double tier rose beds decorated with strewn oyster shells and pebbles shored up by sawn lengths of telegraph poles and heavy wooden beams, a brick walled pathway at the bottom; so much of interest to take in.

'The fish are very big,' said Betty, leaning forward, her expression quizzical as they paused by the lower pond where there was a profusion of yellow lilies, bees buzzing around flower tubs nearby on the patio.

'How they plop about, glide underwater, weaving this way and that. Oh, Mr Cribbins, the water's so clear. Mrs Bunn's pond is all green with algae and choked.'

'Yep, that water feeds from my own well. We'll take a peep at that later, although part of the reason I asked you to come an' see me at the box today, Miss Blake, is because there's a thief about, two of my fine fish gorn. I wonders, knowin' 'ow you is summink of a sleuth, clever at solving village mysteries, yer might look into the matter for me, 'ave a go. Honest, me, I'm fair flummoxed. I kept my eyes peeled for a cat or summat the last few days, but I h'aint seen anyfing.'

'Two fish missing?'

'Two of me fattest 'n finest. Fifteen pound white Koi anna seventeen pounder. Ooh, 'ad 'em for years. Keeps me goldfish an' wild carp in the top pond, see.' Betty Blake agreed to help, of course she did.

'But there's summink else I ain't tol'

another soul. Promise you'll keep a secret, the both of yer.'

'Alright,' said Snark, intrigued, prepared to put scepticism to the wind. 'A promise is a promise,' agreed Betty, meaning every word, for Mr Cribbins the railwayman was such a dear, that she should never dream of betraying his trust.

Seemingly satisfied, the branch signalman replaced his charred tobacco pipe in his mouth. He guided the excited children along the grass, past the patio ornamented with a pair of carved stone Spanish donkeys, the dwarf sized garden hut with asphalt roof, the weather-beaten timber duck house and hatchery, the fruit trees burdened with clusters of apples, plums and pears until they finally reached the circular brick and cemented well, intuitively dug and built by Mr Cribbins single-handedly.

'Pal o' mine,' said he, cheerfully, 'once tol' me, an old wise country fella he were too, a water diviner it so happens, y'know uses a Y-shaped twig, that I'd likely as not struck a fairy spring, the luck I had discovering this source of water too remarkable.

''Mr Openshawe,' I laughed, slapping him on the back, 'enough of blinkin' fairies. I've got me a wonderful free source of pure, fresh water. I'm gonna build me ponds, a miniature water wheel, 'ave a runnin' stream, reed beds and plank bridges. Yes, I've been fortunate, certainly, but fairy folk is takin' it too far. You mean they sort of influenced me, guided me to the spot? Well, I never see'd no fairies, goblins nor elves either in me garden.' My companion showed annoyance at my nonchalant, carefree attitude.

''But you will,' promised he guardedly, and mind I was respectful of Mr Openshawe, I was often privileged to shoot rabbits and pheasants with 'im, for he was head gamekeeper on Sir Winton Clarke's estates. 'Oh yes, the time will come, my lad,' said he emphatically.

'Well, Betty, no sooner had he spoke than I felt a shiver like someone had just walked over me grave. See, I'd read somewhere most fairies were capable of spreading fairy dust and good fortune to

161

us gardeners, but others wilful, spiteful, downright evil causing blight and disease to plants, despising humankind . . . which lot I was lumbered with I paused to wonder, but as time went by and my garden flourished, became a beautiful haven, getting lovelier with each season. I knew in my heart I had been blessed and if, as Mr Openshawe suggested, garden fairies really existed then, why, they and their magical spring were very welcome.'

★　★　★

After going home for a proper tea, the weather being warm and sunny, the children returned that late afternoon to the railway cottage. Although Mr Cribbins must remain on duty at his box as arranged, Betty Blake and the boy, keeping a lookout for possibly a cat or a fox, took up their vantage in the garden greenhouse attached to the cottage, a giant prickly pear cactus for company. There was a splendid view of the upper and lower ponds and the garden in general. What was it Mama, Aunt Medley and Mr Cribbins mentioned in common that day? T'was midsummer's eve . . .

Time passed, but still no sign of a prowler, then at eventide as a glorious silken sunset melted purple, red, the children witnessed the first remarkable happening.

This is no lie, no exaggeration, not made up nor embellished.

A garden ornament, a hand painted footballer, the stone figure left out in the elements for a long time had somehow come alive. Why, he was kicking a fir cone along the grass and such was his deft control, the footballer flicked it first onto his head — *crunk* — bounced it onto his raised knee — *doonk* — and rolled it down his leg — *duggety-duggety, dug-dug* — onto the ground, making a very fine dribble past the greenhouse.

A tiny whistle blew, and yet more granite garden ornaments, this time a steam tractor driven by a hedgehog, towing a tinker's caravan. How was this possible? After all, they were stone and quite heavy. The procession continued, including a pair of stone-age, big-nosed

163

trolls — man and wife, the entwined lovers, the gossips, old Tom, the scold, the snail, the cricketer, the umpire, the demon imp, the Spanish donkeys, once solid stone figures, weighty, inanimate objects, magically transformed, clunking and scraping along merrily, hastening towards the end of the garden.

Meanwhile, high on the corner of the grassy bank a black and white pig, a stone effigy, would keep squealing and grunting, all the ornaments headed in the direction of Mr Cribbins' brick and concreted well. Why, all the garden ornaments it appeared were gathering to celebrate midsummer's eve, joining a host of pretty, fluttering fairies who entwined delicate, gossamer hands and were dancing firstly one way then the other round the well's perimeter, the area lit up by glow worms. Viewed from the greenhouse, the children entranced, brim full of wonder at the spectacle. Gliding from the shadows of the little orchard, the ghostly presence of the deceased, Flora Abingdon, the previous signal-man's wife who had, in life, herself tended this plot of land, although then not so finely developed or planned out. Beside her was the ghost dog Beezer, the Newfoundland. Rather akin to emulsified images upon a glass negative plate, they imposed themselves before the greenhouse, the deceased woman using telepathy for communication mouthed silent yet wise counsel.

'Now dears, not a word to anybody about this. The fairy folk is lovely, ever so kind, but werry strict. Never, never, I say, mention about the magical doings this eventide to no one . . . not even to your mother.'

A tall, spindly, very elderly regal lady, fashionable, a person of means when alive, dressed in only black with a fur stole and ostrich feathered hat, but not a funerary shade sent to scare, else to cause undue fright, loomed behind the signalman's wife importantly, watching the children curiously. She, too, by means of telepathy mouthing the words, politely offered a useful suggestion.

'Betty Blake, take thy lighted oil lamp, child, shine it thus over the still waters of the lower pond. Thus dear you shall catch your cunning thief, the one you seek, unawares. My love to your mother and Aunt Medley.'

★ ★ ★

That evening, the air balmy and warm, buzzing with insects, the chatter of roosting birds evident from the fruit trees, Betty, goggle-eyed, Snark Davis in tow, crept to the edge of the pond and shone the lamp as directed, scanning the smooth, un-rippled surface water fed from the well stream. There, caught by the soft glow radiated from the oil lantern, the undulating fiend, fond of lurking in the reeds and groups of lilies, its long, hideous snout filled with row upon row of vicious sharp teeth. Once caught, stuffed and baked in the oven, the fearsome fish, a freshwater pike, made a very fine supper that Mr Cribbins enjoyed heartily.

What was peculiar to Betty Blake, however, concerned not so much the pike, but the tall, mysterious lady, the woman in black, the ghost who passed on the hint very generously causing the identity of the thief to be revealed, her stern if not unkindly countenance, that prim, wizened old face, the girl recognised from somewhere. But, from where?

Much as she wracked her brains on the way home, it was only when she was once more indoors, ensconced in the brick and timber clad thatched cottage along Old Pasture Lane and about to clean her teeth before going to bed, her observant eye caught sight of a tiny framed sepia photograph on top of Aunt Medley's dressing table as she passed the partly open bedroom door.

It was her, it had to be. She asked Auntie to tell her a little about this formidable old woman in black, whereupon the aunt jogged her memory, reminding her niece she was of course none other than Great, Great Grandmother Cecily who once lived in Balham. Thus the observant, helpful garden ghost and Betty were not only related, but sleuths of a kindred kind.

The Sweep's Tale

Upon the next occasion the Blakes' cottage chimneys needed to be swept of accumulated birds' nests and coal fire debris, Mr Arkwright arrived in jolly form, whistling all the while, pushing his hand cart down the lane loaded with grades of shovel, long-poled brushes, ladders and tarpaulin sheets.

While he took his tea break in the parlour, the sweep related the following true event which occurred when he was but a youth apprenticed to a Mr Todd of Fernley Dole.

'Betty, I was younger then, mebbe fourteen. Fernley Dole is, as you know, a hamlet the other side of Woolminster dominated then, as now, by the big house, a Palladian mansion belonging to the Alford family. Each May us sweeps from the county, a blacker and filthier mob as ever seen at one gathering, got together to bang shovels and hammers, medal lids, creating havoc, following in procession our Jack-o'-the-Green, a tall wicker figure robed in evergreens, crowned by a garland of flowers. The procession included the Giants, the Morris Sides, the Bogeys, Black Sal and Ol' Nick on a donkey.

''The labouring class outreach themselves. I don't want those dirty, stinky fellows, the drunken and disorderly sweeps, parading in our hamlet any more,' said her ladyship one May morn to he who owned all the land and estates for miles, the Lord of the Manor, Henry Alford. ''Tis not Christian — it harks back to a time of green giants, goblins, sacrifice of maidens and worship of pagan gods. You must stop this festival . . . ban it. You *will* stop it, Lord Alford. Fernley Dole must be free of this vile Jack-o'-the-Green excitement, this loathsome tour from one public house to another, both rowdy and lecherous. Well, Henry?'

'You are, of course, right, my dear. I shall put a stop to it this instant.'

'Thus, for the first time in a century or more the parade of the Worshipful

169

Company of Chimney Sweeps was banned and a magistrate's order obtained. What could we do? Them's at the big house could do what they liked, we were just scum. But . . . but Betty, on the eve of Jack-o'-the-Green, a strange fate befell the Lady Alford. For denying our wicker man his yearly outing she paid with her life.

'Mr Todd, my employer, and I were knocked up at the sweep's house, a servant sent by his grieving master to fetch us. What misery, for during the high winds, the gales that raged all day over the county, her ladyship had been seated, as was her custom, before the great fireplace attending to her embroidery when in an instant a tiny skull came hurtling down the chimney, crashing into the grate amongst the burning coals. The skull seemed to grin at her, rapidly growing redder and hotter, glowing the more fiercely in the roaring flame.

'Such was the shock, the Lady Alford collapsed and died on the spot of a heart failure, terror spoiling her once attractive womanly features. I tell you truthfully,

Betty, Lord Alford, now a widower on the eve of Jack-o'-the-Green, showed us the very fireplace, the tiny grinning skull still in place, central to the heaped coal ash.

' ''Tis devilry, sir. What am I to make of this blasphemous monstrosity sent from some pagan realm? Well, Mr Todd, have you any view? My poor deceased wife awaits the vault, resting within her studded lead-lined coffin in the chapel as we speak.'

'Without further ado, Mr Todd charged me, his apprentice, to poke long poles up the chimney and be prepared for a retrieval.

' ''Lord Alford, sir, I offer my condolences,' my employer said, humbly holding his filthy, greasy cap in his even grubbier hands, his clothes and face, like mine, black with coal grime, proud of the fact we hardly ever washed.

' ''I fear, in another age to our own, a master sweep like myself ordered his climbing boy to ascend this vast chimney belonging to your lordship's magnificent Palladian mansion set as it is in acres of park. Alas, the boy became awkwardly stuck, killed by an avalanche of soot, asphyxiating him along one of the bends. May God forgive me,' for he, the master sweep, concerned only with pocketing his fee, not wishing to face criminal proceedings for negligence, nor the bother of knocking a wall down to retrieve the body, bearing in mind the extra cost to his lordship, decides to leave the poor child's corpse high up where it was. Over time it had turned into a decayed skeleton and the high winds finally dislodged the heap of bones, causing the child's skull to fall down the wide chimney into the grate. Lord save us, sir. Bless your lordship. Like your dear departed wife, the Lady Alford, at least bestow a kindly boon. Allow these paltry remains of a destitute pauper a decent Christian burial in yonder green and pleasant churchyard.'

''Zounds,' his lordship sneered, unable to conceal his disapproval, full of utter contempt for such a suggestion. 'On the north side perhaps wherein lie the unmarked graves of paupers, suicides and plague victims; that will do well enough, yet still I have but a wiser course. Let the skeleton be hung whole, wired well, as a classroom exhibit for the betterment of science.''

'Oh, Mr Arkwright,' sighed Betty Blake, enjoying the strange account of true life events. 'I should so like to discover a mysterious skull for myself.'

Lost and Found

Betty Blake was travelling back by train from Woolbridge Halt where there was a gravel pit, and on higher ground, a woodland trail. The local newspaper carried an article that week concerning the Lyminster Archaeological Society which was in the process of carrying out a dig in the area to locate traces of an early Bronze Age settlement. Joining her on the day out to the gravel pit was Winnie White and best friend Lizzie.

Whilst the two carriages with clerestory roofs, a raised central section, compartments lit when dark by compressed oil gas rattled along. Winnie raised her eyes to the luggage rack and for the first time spied an item that must have been left behind by somebody.

'Oh, do look, you lot,' she exclaimed, jumping up, 'a hat box, a pretty ordinary one, somebody left it in the corner, forgot to take it with them. Betty, stand on the seat and fetch it down, we must look inside. Is there a label, a name, something of the owner?'

Clambering over the cloth covered seat, despite the carriage lurching, Betty managed to cling onto the wire rack, stretching out her arm to nudge the hat box further towards her, passing it down carefully to Lizzie, the tallest of the trio who in turn handed it to Winnie, the shortest.

The girls huddled round. Admittedly the hat box looked fairly battered, the outer silk threadbare, worn in places. Winnie, propping her knee on the seat, lifted the hat box lid, everyone eager to see what lay inside — a 'poke' bonnet, a trendy cloche or chimney pot hat like Betty wore? Nothing like that — a human skull . . .

Betty Blake lost no time lifting it out and twirling it round like Hamlet. But, face it, a skull, however hard we try to think about it, looks just like a zillion others buried in cemeteries and church-yards all over Britain. How this one came to be left in a hat box on a passenger train was certainly queer though.

The girls were perhaps naturally inquisitive. Scared? No, definitely not. The sun was shining; it was a lovely summer's day, motes of floating dust, bars of bright sunlight filling the compartment.

'Poor old 'Skully', he looks ever so sorry for himself,' said Winnie, patting the chalky white dome, the cranium.

'That's if it's a 'he' and not a 'she',' pointed out Betty.

She peered at the inner lining of the hat box, noticing paint stains, long dried, most likely caused by a painter's brushes, a palate knife, leaky tubes of paint, so she quickly surmised the hat box could have belonged to an artist travelling on the train, an artist who preferred to paint in oils, carried the old hat box along with a portable easel when outdoors; all speculation, mind.

'I suppose we'd better hand it in at the station, the Parcels Office, Lost Property,' suggested Winnie, anxious to be good and sensible. ''Skully' does look awfully glum.'

Betty had another more daring proposition. 'Hang it all, Winnie. I know just the person who could help. I mean, if it's prehistoric belonging to a hairy chimpman or ape man, whatever.'

'Oh,' exclaimed Lizzie not really sure, replacing the skull in the hat box, for the stopping service was presently coming into Lyminster station. Winnie re-secured the lid, but was more determined than ever to be good, to do right.

'We'd better just hand it in,' said she, primly as could be. 'It's not our property, after all. Someone may want to claim it.'

'No,' insisted Betty. 'We must take it to an expert.'

Once away from the station the girls called to see Professor Lallington, whom Betty knew from 'The Pillar Box Puzzle', when the kindly chappie had been a great help to her, one of his local history books in the public library being crucial to solving a village mystery.

He was, in fact, the nearest personality Betty could equate locally as being akin to A.C. Doyle's Sherlock Holmes. Alright, perhaps an older, salt-and-pepper-haired version. But the professor had the requisite hawk-like features, was very tall and lanky and sometimes wore a dressing gown when pottering around indoors.

His favourite choice of tobacco pipes was a curved meerschaum, the bowl carved in the shape of a gargoyle. Professor Lallington was at home busy writing his next folklore volume, ensconced in his cramped, book-lined study, when the trio called. He welcomed them wholeheartedly, requesting his trusty Mrs Hurlingstone to fetch a cooling jug of Robinson's lemon barley water and the biscuit barrel.

'Now, my dears,' said he, sitting them all down. 'I observe a perfectly ordinary black hat box, somewhat battered, of long usage. However, its contents are, I presume, of singular significance. That's it, drink your barley water. Betty, what have you got to tell me?'

'Well, Professor, we found it on the train. It had been left behind, on the luggage rack.'

'A human skull,' he said, prising off the lid, adjusting his round spectacles. He lit his pipe, pondering the object.

'Is 'Skully' prehistoric?' queried Winnie, politely, putting her empty glass on the arm of the chair.

'Neanderthal? No, I think not. Bronze Age far more of a possibility,' said he, glowering in her direction. 'Yes, upon first impressions it appears so.'

'Could somebody have been travelling with the hat box from the gravel pit?' asked Lizzie.

'Sharp, very astute. You infer an anthropologist, a member of the British Palaeontological community. A plausible theory that holds much merit certainly. But let us consider the skull's actual age. Might I carry out a number of tests, a chemistry experiment, Betty? We must use every method open to us, be unafraid of modernity.'

'Oh, do, please do,' she answered, so delighted to see the gentleman kept a table available over by the window littered with all manner of chemistry paraphernalia — a coloured display of crystals and liquids, racks of oddly shaped crucibles, test tubes, retorts and further useful apparatus, a Bunsen burner close to hand, just like Sherlock at 221B used to create his own stinks. This was just too good to be true. Perhaps she might regard the professor as a close relation to the great consulting detective. Whatever, the girls gathered round to watch. Ten minutes later the professor was ready: 'Humph,' said he, talking more to himself than his captive audience. 'A most edifying development. I concur the skull was cunningly soaked in a solution of potassium dichromate to produce a realistic patina, an aging effect, may even have been boiled in an iron sulphate solution. We can therefore discount its Simian origins as entirely bogus.'

'What does all that mean, please?' asked Lizzie.

'Well, my dear, I believe this to be a human skull closer to our own time, faked to appear much older.'

★　★　★

Professor Lallington wished to perform more tests so it was unanimously agreed he should keep the skull till Monday. He would also make a forensic study of the worn hat box, then all parties should confer as to what further steps should be taken.

Later that evening, the girls were gathered in Betty's bedroom beneath the eves and sweet smelling thatch, the skull mystery becoming more and more intriguing. 'Suppose, just suppose, the hat box belonged to an artist, a painter who used the hat box for convenience sake to store brushes and tubes.'

'Only one way to find out,' admitted Betty, sat upon the edge of her bed. Recalling a Sherlock adventure she had read in Mother's latest edition of the *Strand Magazine*. Maybe she should adopt one of Holmes' tried and tested methods that got results fast. AN ADVERTISEMENT. This one placed in the *Lyminster Echo:*

Lost and Found. Artist's hat box left on train. Please contact Mr Lallington, No. 6 Old Pasture Lane for safe return.

On the Tuesday, a lady called at the professor's country cottage. She was refined, elegant and impeccably turned out. She was a professional artist, a member of the Royal Academy who had enjoyed exhibitions both here and abroad; her name Maggie Swinfen.

'Oh, how kind of you, silly me. I was weighed down with shopping bags and totally forgot my old hat box. I left it on the rack the other day. Let's see, a shilling each. Thank the girls ever so for bothering. My friend Mr Hoad lent me the artefact for a composition I intend to sketch. The skull has been in his family for years. A notorious hoax whereby his naughty great grandfather attempted to dupe the Natural History Society, fobbing it off as a genuine prehistoric find, when in point of fact it was a fake. He was deservedly rapped on the knuckles and suffered ridicule from fellow club members for many years afterwards.'

Other titles in the
Linford Mystery Library:

THE SEVENTH VIRGIN

Gerald Verner

When Constable Joe Bentley rescues what he thinks is a nude woman from the freezing waters of the River Thames, his catch turns out to be an exquisitely modelled tailor's dummy stuffed with thousands of pounds' worth of bank notes. Later that same morning, the dead body of a man is found further downriver. Superintendent Budd of Scotland Yard, under pressure to prevent millions of counterfeit notes from entering general circulation, must discover the connection between the incidents, and stop a cold-blooded murderer on a killing spree.

A NICE GIRL LIKE YOU

Richard Wormser

Lt. Andy Bastian is back for his second scintillating case. This time, he heads a gritting and gruesome search for the man who violated a teenage beauty and left her just intact enough to someday tell the tale. But when his best friend becomes the number one suspect in the case, Andy becomes one of the star legal attractions. Without an alibi, things look bad for Andy's friend — but can Andy offer to help him and keep his integrity intact?

THE BALLAD OF THE RUNNING MAN

Shelley Smith

On the Alps, two schoolteachers discover a gruesome sight — the corpse of a murdered man. How the corpse came to be there is the story of Rex Buchanan and his wife Paula. Rex, a pulp fiction author, comes home one day eager to tell Paula about a fantastic plot for his next novel, *The Ballad of the Running Man*. A man insures his life, and with the aid of his wife pretends to fall ill and eventually 'dies' — but Rex wants them to act it out in real life . . .

THE HANGING HEIRESS

Richard Wormser

Marty Cockren, ex-newspaper man and rookie private detective, is offered the chance to earn big money acting as bodyguard to beautiful young widow Eve Chounet, who is due to inherit a huge fortune from her late husband — though as a caveat, only if she remains alive for thirty days, whilst delivering his portrait paintings to each of his companies. But the principals of some of those companies are hell-bent on her murder, and Marty must use all of his cunning to stay ahead of the individuals involved and keep Eve alive . . .

UNDERCURRENT OF EVIL

Norman Firth

After Sheila Nesbitt's father is found dead in the Thames following a visit to the Satyr Club, the most exclusive gambling parlour in town, she's determined to uncover the truth of what happened. Enlisting the help of her friend, Richard Denning, they set out to investigate what grim secrets the Satyr Club is hiding behind the suave smile of the manager, Collwell, and his sultry, seductive assistant, Lady Mercia Standard, who sets her sights on Richard. Their pursuit eventually leads them to the club's mysterious owner — 'The Old Devil'.